AGE SMART

How to Age Well, Stay Fit and Be Happy

Harriet M. Vines, Ph.D.

Llumina Press

Other Books by Dr. Vines

Bridges to Success with Dr. Margaret F. Austin

Get That Job with Dr. Margaret F. Austin

Requests for permission to make copies of any part of this work should be mailed to Permissions Department, Llumina Press, PO Box 772246, Coral Springs, FL 33077-2246

ISBN: 978-1-59526-741-2

Printed in the United States of America by Llumina Press

Library of Congress Control Number: 2007900648

FYI: BUSINESS, INDUSTRIAL, EDUCATION, HEALTH & SOCIAL ORGANIZATIONS, PUBLICATIONS & ASSOCIATIONS: Quantity discounts are available on bulk purchases of this book for reselling, educational purposes, incentives, premiums, gifts, or fund raising. Special excerpts or covers can be created to meet specifications. For information, please contact Age Smart® Associates, POB 561, Lenox MA 01240, 413.637.4036

Praise for AGE SMART

I can't stop myself from aging, but I certainly can age smart. This easy to read book has many practical, positive and invaluable ideas on how I, like wine, can age well. *Age Smart* is a "how to" book which empowers and inspires readers to age successfully and happily.

Helene L. Calman, Psychotherapist

Age Smart is a timely, effective 'must read,' filled with vital information and techniques for readers who want to continue to live meaningful, productive lives.

Dr. Harry A. Galinsky, Superintendent of Schools, Ret.; Educational Advisor to Presidents Ronald Reagan and George H. Bush

A valuable, comprehensive resource for dealing with the challenges of aging. *Age Smart* covers the broad range of emotional, physical and psychological issues specific to this age group. I highly recommend it.

Lenore Greenstein, R.D., M.Ed. Director, Title 3-C Nutrition Program for the Elderly; Consultant, Canyon Ranch Health Spa; Columnist, Naples Daily News

Dr. Vines has written a compendium of useful information, tips and sound advice for achieving and maintaining good health while we age. The *Age Smart* approach - a positive "take charge" life style with emphasis on continued learning and maintenance of mental acuity - can certainly help to mitigate some negative concomitants of aging. Her chapters on nutrition, exercise and fitness are important indeed.

Irving Kronenberg, MPA, President, CEO Hebrew Home & Hospital, West Hartford, CT Ret.; Medical School Faculty, Univ. CT, Brown, NYU, SUNY Downstate; Founder Hospice Care, R.I.

An important book for mature adults and those who care about them. *Age Smart* provides a wealth of easy to understand information about how to develop and maintain physical health and mental fitness as people age. The exercises are imaginative, stimulating and fun to do.

Stephen Radin, Education Consultant

This is an important book for all of us fortunate enough to be aging. Everyone can benefit from its exercises to maintain and even increase mental abilities and functioning. Dr. Vines' emphasis on the mind/body connection is critical to healthy aging. *Age Smart* is a major contribution to the field of health and wellness.

Lenore Borzak Rubin, Ph.D. Author; Consultant, Management and Executive Coaching to NYNEX, Crane & Co., Mead Papers, KB Toys

Dr. Harriet Vines' most recent course, "Age Smart, Age Happy," for The Berkshire Institute for Lifetime Learning, a recognized program of educational opportunities for mature learners, was exceptionally well received. Member comments were filled with praise. Fortunately, she has expanded her guidelines further in this book, which should prove to be a valued addition to this important field.

Arthur Sherman, BILL Curriculum Committee Chair and Past President

Truly this is no ordinary book of truisms and platitudes. *Age Smart* is a greatly nuanced display of the vital mind/body link and aging process. It is user-friendly, exudes wisdom and compassion throughout, and advocates mindfulness in all aspects of living. I have lived actively into my ninth decade and recommend this book without reservation.

Ira A. Wasserberg, M.D., FACS, Diplomate of the American Board of Urology; Associate Professor, New York University/Bellevue Medical Center

"Age Smart" presentations have wowed residents and professional audiences for many years. Some exercises may seem rigorous, but the outcome is worth it. Harriet Vines is a great example of someone who is aging smart; she is aging well, staying fit, and sure seems happy!

Diane I. Weinstein, OTR/L, MSPA, Executive Director, Nationally Owned Assisted Living Community

ACKNOWLEDGEMENTS

To the many workshop participants and adult ed students who generously shared stories, insights and sage advice.

To Shirley Blanchard and Helen Radin for their much appreciated, valuable editorial assistance.

To Elliott Vines, companion, helpmate and best friend, 52 years and counting. Come along with me, lots of good stuff is yet to be (with all due respect to R. Browning).

CONTENTS

INTRODUCTION

New perspectives opened for me when I retired early from my position as Associate Professor, York College and creator of the Big Apple Job Fair, The City University of New York. Intrinsically motivated, I began to explore and research the stage of life I was now in.

To my chagrin, most of what I found concerned the health, housing, financial, and disability problems faced by far too many people, but little that addressed normal age-appropriate concerns of healthy, mature men and women, like you and me. Yet, *we are the majority in this age group.*

The attention and publicity paid to the difficult problems some people encounter as they age foster the impression that aging is all-negative, all the time. But we know that isn't so.

Yes, there are significant problems, but there are serious problems at every age. We've known them; we've lived them. We've also lived and known ourselves to be loving, capable, responsible, problem solving individuals. More importantly - *we still see ourselves that way.*

We're effectively functioning adults, thank you very much, and we intend to keep leading productive, meaningful, Happy (*sic*) lives.

Unfortunately, too many unflattering jokes and Shakespeare's put down "...second childishness and mere oblivion; Sans teeth, sans eyes, sans taste, sans everything" (*As You Like It*) are still out there working against us.

But my studies clearly showed each of us has the ability, through our brainpower, to contravene the stereotype, i.e., to age well.

Age Smart is the extension of my firm belief, based on research reinforced by empirical evidence, that it is *never* too late to grow the mind. Sharpened mental fitness coupled with an appropriate life style give us the power to shape the way we age.

I developed the *Age Smart* mental fitness program to share these important findings. This book is my effort *a*) to reach and support more of the majority, my peers who want to exert control over the way they age, *b*) to reinforce their determination to age well and *c*) to offer a viable way to accomplish their objectives.

Remember, it's not *what* age you are that matters, it's *how* you age. Be proactive. Take charge.

Age the way you want to be: Smart, Well, Fit, and Happy.

Harriet Vines

There is a fountain of youth. It is your mind, your talents, the creativity you bring to your life. Tap this source, and you defeat age.

Sophia Loren

How old would you be if you didn't know how old you were?

Satchel Paige

I could not, at any age, be content to take my place by the fireside and simply look on.

Eleanor Roosevelt

Age is of no importance unless you are a cheese.

Anonymous

1

AGE WELL

How do you cope with today's extended life expectancy, age effectively and stay in control of your life? Back in 1711 Jonathan Swift, author of *Gulliver's Travels*, observed, "every one desires to live long, but no one would be old."

Three hundred years later, that's still true. But how is it possible? How do you live longer and *not* 'grow old'? The answer is to age pro-actively: *Age Smart*.

HOW DO YOU AGE SMART?

- ❖ You *Age Smart* when you use your brain to age well.
- ❖ You *Age Smart* when you take advantage of the latest research on aging.
- ❖ You *Age Smart* when you do the many things you have control over and the power to do to age successfully.
- ❖ You *Age Smart* when you practice positive psychology.
- ❖ You *Age Smart* when you become and remain physically and mentally fit, the *sine qua non,* the bottom line, of positive aging.

IT'S YOUR CALL

At the turn of the millennium, "fitness" was the buzzword. Millions of women and men exercised, watched their diet and considered themselves fit.

Today, however, we know more. We know "total fitness" denotes physical *and mental* fitness. We recognize the mind/body connection and use the mind's ability to control the body to our advantage, to exert control over the way we age.

The MacArthur Foundation Study of Successful Aging, the respected in-depth investigation of the aging process, identifies three fundamental components of aging well:

1.   A low risk of debilitating disease
2.   Physical and mental fitness
3.   Social interaction

Your mind enables you to control all three factors.

The results of the *MacArthur Foundation Study* reveal that many of the complaints people attribute to "old age" actually result from the life style they've chosen, e.g., not enough exercise, poor nutrition, not much socializing. Evidence indicates the way people age depends primarily on personal decisions, choices and actions, all products of conscious, self-directed mental activity.

If you choose to age well and happy, put your mind to work at learning how to do it. You can guide the process.

**Determinants of
Successful Aging**

√ Low Risk of Debilitating Disease
√ Physical and Mental Fitness
√ Social Interaction

Victor Frankl, holocaust concentration camp survivor and existential psychologist, maintained we can't control everything that happens to us, but we can determine our stance in a given set of circumstances. That's mind work. Your brain has the power to do that.

For example, your behavior, more than any other factor, influences your general resistance to disease. Sir William Osler, a physician and professor of medicine at the turn of the 19th century, used to say it was more important to know what kind of patient had the disease than what kind of disease the patient had.

People who are disease resistant have a positive outlook. They are concerned about others and see themselves as being in control, rather than as victims of circumstance. They perceive challenges not as threats, but as opportunities to grow and learn.

Resistance to disease is driven by attitude. And so is aging - driven by attitude. It's tricky because you've not done it before, and there haven't been many role models. But your mental take on aging tells a lot about how you handle the process.

What kind of self-fulfilling prophecies do you set up? Do you tend to be optimistic, or is your glass the half empty one? A more positive outlook feeds happiness.

With the right attitude, you can take charge of your health and fitness and manage your social activities. You can choose to get your mind in shape.

No matter your age, mental improvement is possible. The sooner you start, the longer you benefit. Your mind has the capacity to grow and learn, to rise to the challenges you offer it - at any age. In fact, it welcomes challenge - that's what keeps it from going flat.

You are responsible for your own aging.

OVERVIEW

❖ *Age Smart* corrects for distortion the myths about aging that may interfere with your doing all you can and should do to age effectively.
❖ *Age Smart* shows how mental fitness drives aging well.
❖ *Age Smart* clarifies how you shape the aging process.
❖ *Age Smart* gives you the skills and tools needed to age pro-actively.

❖ *Age Smart* helps you improve your memory and keep it strong.
❖ *Age Smart* explains how to follow the principles of positive psychology that promote happiness.

The future is longer than ever. Life expectancy for people born today is 77.6 years. The fastest growing age group in the United States is 100+. People who are sixty-five today can expect to live another 18-20 years. That's great, you say; however....

However, by now you know enough to want those years to be rewarding, to add up to meaningful, quality time. You want to feel good and enjoy life. You want to be Happy (*sic*). That's only natural. You come programmed with a desire for happiness. Happiness is so important to your well being that your brain is hardwired to make you feel happy. It has built-in pathways and neural transmitters designed for that purpose.

From the beginning of recorded time, the desire to be happy has been universal. The philosophers of the Enlightenment believed the best society is one where the citizens are happiest, and therefore, the best public policy is one that produces the greatest happiness for the greatest number. This spirit appears in the U.S. Declaration of Independence as the self-evident truth of our unalienable right to pursue happiness.

However, the Happiness we seek, the one with a capital H, is more than casual have-a-nice-day pleasant feelings or momentary enjoyments and transitory pleasures - though no one denies their worth. Happy moments bestow emotional value and physical benefits. We feel wonderful. But they're too fleeting, they're not enough. It's strategic to look for something more substantial and authentic (See Chapter 3).

THE GAME PLAN

Currently, there are 60,000-80,000 centenarians in the U.S. Knowing you could live to be 100 may sound good, but it also could seem a mixed blessing. On the one hand, it's welcome news. Like most people, you probably like the idea of living to the proverbial "ripe old age." On the other, it could be a little anxiety producing. It sounds good, but only under certain circumstances, i.e., only if you can avoid the discomforts attributed to aging and can continue to be yourself as you see yourself. You don't want to worry about losing your physical and mental prowess.

You will be pleased to know diminished mental acuity is *not* a necessary part of aging. Studies at Duke University and the National Institute on Aging (NIA) have shown that mental and physical decline, often associated with aging, are neither probable nor inevitable. You will be reassured to know fewer than ten percent of people under 75 years of age have Alzheimer's disease or any form of dementia.

Like most people, you want to be able to understand and remember the things you do, places you go and people you meet. You want to be able to concentrate on the book you're reading, the TV program you're watching or the movie you're seeing. You want to be able to talk to friends about them without forgetting names and blocking words.

You don't want to avoid social situations because you lack confidence in your cognitive capacity. You want to feel comfortable about meeting people and holding up your end of the conversation. You want to be secure about managing your affairs and confident in your ability to handle yourself well. You want to be purposefully engaged.

You can do all these good things. *Age Smart* empowers you to age successfully. You will learn to exert control over the way you age. Your brain is team captain. It regulates your body systems and manages your mental functions. The mind is what the brain does; training strengthens this dynamic duo. And therein lies your power.

Your brain can be trained, so train it. Increase your awareness of it, learn how to use your brain to manage the aging process and strengthen your ability to age well.

Use your "master muscle" to make your life more satisfying, productive, meaningful, and enjoyable. No matter what anyone says or advertisements imply, you cannot stop aging, but it is within your power to shape the way you process it. You have the power to increase your mental fitness. The brain's job is to mind the body; your job is to mind your brain.

But you can't do it all at once. Just the fact you are reading *Age Smart* is a step in the right direction. The changes you make in your mind and body will make you want to do more. Each small success leads on to the next.

Try this now. Look around. See if you can spot five blue objects small enough to fit into your pocket and five red ones that are too big. There! You just did an exercise that strengthened your powers of observation. Improving and maintaining your mental fitness can be as simple as that.

Here's the Game Plan: Take care of your brain as well as you take care of your body. Just as you exercise to strengthen your body's muscles to keep physically fit, you should exercise your brain's muscles to stay mentally fit.

You don't even have to go to a health club. Do the *Mental Fitness Workout (MFW)* in each chapter. *MFWs* are winning plays that promote successful aging.

It is never too late to start nor too soon to begin doing them. The earlier, the better - the greater the benefit. The more fit your brain, the greater your mental acuity. Since your mind enables you to control the way you age, flexing your brain's muscles will fortify the skills you need to maintain control.

Dr. Gary W. Small, Director of the UCLA Center on Aging and specialist in the early detection and prevention of Alzheimer's disease, notes it is "easier to protect a healthy brain" than try to repair a damaged one.

Evidence is growing that maintaining physical and mental fitness reduces the risk of Alzheimer's disease. Moreover, in an experiment with Alzheimer patients, neuroscientist Ryuta Kawashima, M.D. found mental exercises successfully delayed deterioration of their cognitive functioning.

Chapters 2-7 coach you on how to increase the odds of aging well. You will learn how you can ward off disease and disabling conditions by changing your life style. You will uncover myths that interfere with your controlling the way you age. You will learn about the new integrated approach to diet and exercise, better understand the importance of social interaction and acquire tools to improve your memory. In addition, you will identify your personal strengths and character traits and learn how to capitalize on them to create a life worth living, the primary descriptor of a Happy life.

You can rejuvenate your brain. Keep your brain functions engaged and challenged to prevent memory loss, ward off sluggish thinking and remain alert.

An NIA funded study reported in the December 2006 *Journal of the American Medical Association* indicated even brief (10 sessions) "mental training" improves cognitive functioning. Even more notable was the finding that training results were still present five years later.

Just as you maintain physical strength and fitness through proper diet and exercise, you also should maintain *mental* strength and fitness through proper diet and *mental* exercise. The Fitness Finals in Chapter 8 will help you be a winner.

MENTAL FITNESS WORKOUTS

To help you train for the Fitness Finals, each chapter of *Age Smart* features a *Mental Fitness Workout*. Like physical workouts, *MFWs* enhance conditioning. The exercises and activities are designed to strengthen specific mental muscles and foster mental fitness, hold your attention and enthusiasm and make you smile and think.

Each *MFW* begins with a Relaxation Warm-up and continues with fun-to-do Mental Calisthenics. Interesting and enjoyable exercises follow.

MFW

Warm-ups

Aerobics

Calisthenics

Sensory Drills

Sensory Drills sharpen acuity. Isometrics enhance Perception. Visualization aids organization and recall. Sprints speed processing. Mental Gymnastics increase flexibility. Resistance Training adds strength and endurance. Mental Aerobics build language and association skills. Weight Lifting solidifies coordination. Stretching expands parameters, and Conscious Recall affords needed practice. Each *MFW* ends with a creative Cool-down.

Resist-ance   Visual-ization   Weight Lifting   Stretching

Recall   Isomet-rics   Cool Down   Sprints

You don't have to buy an outfit or carry a gym bag to do an *MFW*, but it is advisable to dress comfortably and work out in a well-lighted setting. You will need pencils, an eraser and a lose-leaf or spiral notebook to record observations and responses and to track your progress. Title the notebook your *Mental Fitness Journal* (MFJ).

Several exercises have three levels of difficulty, indicated by $\sqrt{}$, $\sqrt{}\sqrt{}$, and $\sqrt{}\sqrt{}\sqrt{}$ check marks. Begin at the simplest level the first time you attempt them. Increase the level of difficulty on any repetition to maintain the challenge. Advance at a pace that feels comfortable to you.

Some exercises involve only mental work. A bonus of these mini-mental-massages is you can repeat them - or variations - any time, anywhere for beneficial fun. Give yourself lots of bonuses. You've earned them.

Exercises that ask you to visualize, use your non-dominant hand or do things differently from the way you usually do, enhance flexibility. They create new, different neural pathways and synapses and break stodgy mental habits. Your brain thrives on this.

You probably will enjoy doing some types of exercises more than others, but none are tricky or too difficult. Just follow the directions.

Here are a couple of tips for handling the unfamiliar. 1) Make associations, i.e., relate the new to what you know. 2) When your usual approach to something isn't working, try a different way; aim for flexibility.

The duration of *MFWs* vary because some exercises may need to be done at certain locations or with other people. In timed exercises, respond as rapidly as you can to give your brain a good processing workout. When working with numbers, it is especially important to work as quickly as possible. You activate larger portions of your brain that way.

However, it's important not to try to do too much at any one time. Mental muscles respond more effectively and grow stronger if you *do less more often*. If you begin to tire, lose concentration or interest, take a break; continue when you feel refreshed and ready.

Consistency and continuity are paramount. Establish a routine. Decide which days you will work out, the time you will begin, and try to keep to it.

The best time to do an *MFW* is in the morning when your brain usually functions most effectively and you are probably fresh, alert and able to pay full attention. Don't exercise on an empty stomach; you need energy.

Before you begin exercising, do a quick emotional check. Rapidly assess your anxiety, irritation, depression, and energy levels. Become aware of the impact moods can have on your mental fitness.

Take as long as necessary to attentively complete each *MFW*. Within a short time you will be able to pace yourself, know how much to do and know when it's time for you to rest. It will not take long before you begin to notice improvements in your mental fitness. The amount of benefit you derive varies with the amount of effort you expend, the regularity of your regimen, your diligence, and your willingness to stretch your mental muscles. It's always your call.

No one can do it for you, and no one can make you do it. All it takes is desire, determination and commitment on your part. It is well within your power to strengthen your mental fitness as you age and, thus, your ability to age well.

Aim to complete an *MFW* each week. Think of it as giving yourself a present. Be good to yourself for a month. You'll see progress and want to continue.

MFWs are fun, informative and empowering. You'll be glad you do them.

AGE SMART

MENTAL FITNESS WORKOUT *# 1*

RELAXATION WARM-UP

MFWs begin the same way physical workouts do - with a warm-up - and for the same reason. All muscles work more smoothly when they've been loosened up.

The easiest way to relax your mind is to relax your body, and the easiest way to do that is simply tell your body to relax. Your body listens to your mind; you will feel it happen. It's simply the mind/body connection at work.

After mentally telling your body to relax, you're going to breathe slowly and steadily, take a tension inventory of your body and release any tightness you feel. Mental imaging will complete the warm-up. It only takes a few moments to relax. Read the instructions below completely. Don't begin the warm-up until after you read "Warm up now."

<u>To Relax</u>: Sit comfortably. Unclasp your hands. Leave them open on your lap or at your sides. Keep your legs and ankles uncrossed. Close your eyes. Send a mental message telling your body to relax. Allow it to happen. You will be able to feel the softening.

Do a mental check and release any tension stored in those stress warehouses everybody has: Drop your shoulders, rotate your neck, un-furrow your brow, let your mouth go slack, don't grit your teeth, unclench your jaws, relax your hands, fingers, feet, and toes. Inventory your body, and relax any residual tension.

Next, slowly and deeply inhale and exhale. Silently count ten inhales from 1-10, then ten exhales from 10-1. Keep your eyes closed, and visualize the sky. Consider any thoughts that may occur as clouds, and let them float by. Like clouds, some fleeting thoughts may be fast, some slow, some light and puffy, some dark and stormy. Don't try to stop or focus on any of them. Let them just come and go. When you feel totally relaxed and ready to work out, open your eyes, begin your calisthenics and continue with the exercises that follow.

Warm up now.

MENTAL CALISTHENICS

Mental calisthenics are designed, like jumping jacks at the gym, to get the blood flowing and develop vigor. They should be done immediately following the warm-up. Like all the exercises, they vary in each *MFW*.

Fortunately, you can also do mental calisthenics whenever you have a few extra minutes - standing on a line, riding in a bus, or waiting till the rain stops. Do them any time, anywhere.

C 1a Count aloud as quickly as you can.

Up by 1, down by 1
1, 2, 3, 4, 5 ... 100
100, 99, 98, 97, 96 ... 1

C 1b Say the alphabet aloud. Now say it aloud backwards. Mentally count the number of printed capital letters in the alphabet with curved lines. Enter your answer in your MFJ.

SENSORY DRILLS

Your five senses provide most of the data your brain works on during its waking hours. Keep them in top shape; they're closely tied to memory. If the input isn't accurate and dependable, both mental acuity and memory suffer. Sharpening sensory acuity correlates with increasing your powers of observation. The more observant and accurate you are, the more valid and reliable the data your brain has to work with, and the more vivid, lasting and retrievable your memories.

V 1 Try to see examples or find pictures of $\sqrt{4}$, $\sqrt{\sqrt{7}}$, $\sqrt{\sqrt{\sqrt{10}}}$ of each day's objects indicated below. Feel free to use printed material, TV and the internet. Copy the headings below and list the objects you see under them in your MFJ.

Mon.	Tues.	Wed.	Thurs.	Fri.
Flowers	Gems	Metals	Veggies	Fabrics

A 1 Select the name of a well-known person or a personal acquaintance. Count the number of times you hear the name mentioned in $\sqrt{10}$, $\sqrt{\sqrt{15}}$, $\sqrt{\sqrt{\sqrt{20}}}$ minutes. Enter the name, number of times heard and the amount of time you listened in your MFJ.

ISOMETRICS

I 1 How Many Squares Do You See?

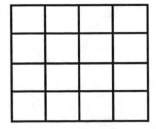

Write the number of squares in your MFJ.

VISUALIZATION

Vz 1 Visualize your childhood bedroom. Next, draw the floor plan. Add furniture, lamps, fixtures, decorations, floor coverings, window treatments, wall hangings, etc. Use colored pencils/crayons. Draw according to a scale you devise.

SPRINTS

Sp 1 Name as many musical instruments as you can in one minute.

MENTAL GYMNASTICS

MG 1 In your MFJ, make a chain of $\sqrt{4}$, $\sqrt{\sqrt{6}}$, $\sqrt{\sqrt{\sqrt{8}}}$ names in which the last syllable of one name becomes the first syllable of the next.

Example: Ellen - Leonard - Ardsley – Leila – Larry

RESISTANCE TRAINING

RT 1 Watch the second hand on a clock sweep around for a full minute - without thinking of anything. If a thought occurs, block it out. Work up to $\sqrt{2}$, $\sqrt{\sqrt{3}}$, $\sqrt{\sqrt{\sqrt{4}}}$ full minutes of watching without letting a thought cross your mind.

MENTAL AEROBICS

MA 1 Copy the pairs of words below into your MFJ, and study them for 10 seconds. In less than one minute, write a word that can be associated with both members of the pair. Example: Plant ---- Book: <u>Leaf</u>

TREE	WORD	INK	PIG
NAILS	RECORDS	PENCIL	PILLOW
FISH	JUSTICE	THEATRE	BIRD

WEIGHT LIFTING

WL 1 Practice synthesizing, a major component of logic; structure a whole from its components. Written below are several well-known proverbs jumbled up. Rewrite them correctly in your MFJ. Explain what they mean.

> Example: bird - the - worm - early - The - catches
> "<u>The early bird catches the worm.</u>" <u>Don't procrastinate</u>.

√ not - Waste - not - want
  root - of - Money - all - the - evil - is
  no- stone - moss - A - gathers – rolling

√√ nine - alone - laughs - A - the - you - saves - cry - world - cry - stitch - and - Laugh - time - you - with- in - you – and

√√√ laughs - glitters - tell - best - gold - by - a - can't - He - laughs - is - All - cover - You - not - who - that- book - last – its

STRETCHING

St 1 Carefully examine a newspaper or magazine photograph for 20 seconds. Then tell the story of the photograph as though you were a radio news broadcaster; then a TV anchor.

CONSCIOUS RECALL

CR 1 Use the speed dial feature on your telephone less often. Learn the telephone numbers you use frequently and dial them from memory.

COOL DOWN

All behavior is goal directed. If you don't know where you're heading, how will you know when you get there? How can you tell if you're making progress?

1. Talk to yourself about why you are reading *Age Smart*. Envision yourself "aging well." What does that mean to you? What images come to mind? What is life like? What is definitely not part of the

picture? Include physical, mental, emotional, social, and financial dimensions. Use your own and others' experiences to inform your reflections. In your MFJ, complete the following thought: I would consider myself to be "aging well" if..................

2. Think carefully about the benefits you would like to gain from doing *Mental Fitness Workouts*. Begin to identify your objectives. In your MFJ, set up a chart similar to the sample that follows. Identify your *Age Smart* goals. Indicate your current status in the appropriate column. Date your entries. Use the sample as a guide.

My Age Smart Goals – Sample

DATE	GOALS	UNSAT.	NEEDS WORK	IMPROVING	OK
1/20	Focus attention more easily for longer time		X		
"	Be more observant in groups	X			
"	Listen better	X			
"	Think more clearly		X		
"	Improve strength and balance	X			
"	Eat less	X			
"	Eat healthier foods		X	X	
"	Strengthen memory		X		
"	Get involved in something	X			
"	Have hearing checked	X			

MENTAL MIGHT

Everyone knows about physical fitness. Its significance and value have been long proven and well documented. Millions of people exercise regularly to get and keep their bodies in shape. You may be one of them. If so, great. Keep it up. It's that important. But how many people do you know who exercise regularly to get and keep their brains in shape?

Yet it is every bit as important. In fact, mental exercise may have an even greater payoff than physical exercise. Don't forget the NIA study that demonstrated only 10 mental workouts were enough to register measurable differences five years later. What physical exercise can make that claim?

MENTAL FITNESS

Total fitness means physical *and* mental fitness. The mind is like the body; if it doesn't get the exercise it needs, it gets out of shape. It gets out of shape when you stop challenging it. You create your own world through your mind. That world gets awfully flat when you don't exercise your mental muscles. Studies at the *Centre de Psychologie Appliquée* in France clearly indicate targeted mental exercises have a positive effect on mental fitness.

What is mental fitness? How does it feel? What does it look like? When we say someone is "mentally fit," what does it mean? How do we recognize it? Like Supreme Court Justice Potter Stewart, who said he couldn't define "pornography" but knew it when he saw it, you know mental fitness when you see it in action. Mental fitness is a construct for the behaviors listed below.

Mentally Fit People

- **Pay attention**
- **Get feedback from the effect of their behavior on others**
- **Consider other people's thoughts and feelings**
- **Are open to new ideas**
- **Perceive change more as challenge than threat**
- **Respond creatively to challenge**
- **Attempt to overcome obstacles, solve problems**
- **Communicate effectively**
- **Use both sides of their brain**
- **Help memory with numerous, innovative links**
- **Listen well**
- **Empathize**
- **Anticipate the results of their actions and others' responses**
- **Process data rationally**
- **Think logically**
- **Have good memories**
- **Are not rigid**
- **Accept constructive criticism**
- **Tolerate differences**

You may be reading *Age Smart* because you understand that mental exercise enhances mental fitness. You may be a reader because you've noticed some words don't come as trippingly to the tongue as they used to, or at times you may feel a touch unsure, out of focus. That's not like you, you don't like it and you're not going to take it any more. You even may be worried that occasional fuzzy-mindedness now could be a sign of more serious problems yet to come.

Losing your mental prowess would be devastating, but as noted above, it does not have to happen. Diminished mental acuity is not an inevitable consequence of living longer. You can take steps to protect yourself against dementia, maintain your independence and hinder cognitive decline.

Just as there are exercises you do to strengthen the muscles of your body, there are exercises you should do to strengthen the muscles of your mind. The evidence at the Mount Sinai Memory and Aging Research Center suggests exercising your brain may reduce the risk of getting Alzheimer's disease or delay the onset.

YOUR MENTAL MUSCLES

The building blocks of mental fitness are Perception, Attention, Endurance, Organization, Flexibility, Coordination, and Conscious Recall. These are the "mental muscles" your mind flexes to do its work. They represent qualities you want to keep strong because you need them to anticipate, solve problems, create, communicate, and remember.

The brain uses these muscles to perform the executive functions we take for granted and dread losing. Mental muscles enable you to think logically, use language, perform spatial manipulations, link associations, make decisions and judgments, and innovate. They also constitute the building blocks your brain uses as a foundation to support memory. Strong mental muscles equal mental fitness.

Your Mental Muscles

PERCEPTION	Sensory acuteness
ATTENTION	The ability to focus, concentrate
ENDURANCE	Persistence; the stamina to sustain an activity, to stay at a job until it's done
ORGANIZATION	Association by logic and intuition
FLEXIBILITY	Open mindedness and creativity
COORDINATION	Reasoning and problem solving
CONSCIOUS RECALL	The ability to locate and retrieve stored data

PERCEPTION is registering and interpreting input from your senses. Look at the figures below.

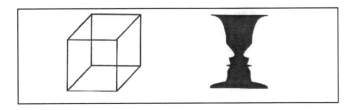

What do you see? The three dimensional cube on the left can alternate between two versions; the figure on the right, between a vase and facing profiles. Both demonstrate the tricks perception plays. Can you make them switch before your eyes?

Aside from thoughts, subconscious messages and autonomic body signals, data from your five senses, vision, hearing, smell, taste, and touch, provide the raw material your mind works with. Your senses are the source of all the stimuli that connect you to the world. It is vital to keep them sharp and reawaken any dulled ones.

Not only do they bring you the data your brain computes and stores in memory, your senses are the source of valuable clues that facilitate recall. Sensory Drills and Isometric exercises will help you keep your senses acute and perceptions accurate.

ATTENTION could be called the most important mental muscle. Without paying attention, perceptions fail to register, register faintly, incorrectly, or not at all. It is difficult to be mentally alert when data are not fully acquired. One problem, however, is attention wanders so easily.

Actually, it's wired to do just that. Attention is programmed to contribute to your sense of continuity and place. Therefore, it roams - sometimes aimlessly - muses, reflects, anticipates, and recalls. This constant shifting is what makes it so hard to stay focused, but you have to resist attention's wandering ways.

As a case in point, try to add this column of figures while you sing *Happy Birthday.*

$$24$$
$$38$$
$$52$$
$$75$$
$$\underline{97}$$

As you clearly see, trying to do two things at the same time interferes with your ability to pay attention to or do either well. Moreover, it becomes more difficult to multitask as you age.

It's not that you can't remember where you left your keys; it's likely you weren't paying attention when you put them down. **Paying attention does more to improve memory** than just about anything else you can do. Resistance Training exercises will increase your ability to focus your attention.

To help you get in the habit of paying attention, start recording your daily activities in your MFJ. Note times you are pleased with your mental performance as well as incidents of mental laxity and/or forgetfulness.

Keeping such notes gets you to focus your awareness and concentration. It makes you PAY ATTENTION to your actions and thoughts and to what is happening about you.

Writing involves thinking, recall and physical reinforcement. The combination increases the likelihood of remembering. Busy people do it all the time. They appreciate having a convenient record of their activities. It is not a sign of weakness. It is not a crutch. It's *smart.*

In time management and organization workshops, participants are urged to use appointment books and calendars as reminders of future events. Use your MFJ log as a reminder of past events.

Keep the log daily until you get into the habit of paying more attention to what you are doing and what is going on around you. It may take 1-2 weeks, maybe longer, but you will begin to notice how much more attentive you become – and how less likely you are to forget where your glasses or car keys are.

Look at the sample below, and begin to keep your log in your MFJ. If you find the log a valuable tool and continue to keep one, you probably will work with larger blocks of time and note only major activities.

		Mental Fitness Log - *Sample*	
Day	Date	Time	Activities
Tues.	4/25	8 - 8:30 am	Stretch & toning exercises; felt a little sluggish
		8:30 - 8:50	Shower & dress
		8:50 - 9:15	Breakfast - all grain cereal, banana, milk
		9:30 - 10:30	Marketing, errands. Remembered item not on list. Yes!!
		11 - 11:45	Began Age Smart. Did relaxation warm-up & calisthenics. Fun. Think I can get it. Began this log.
		12-1:15 pm	Lunch; new veggie soup not great
		1:30 - 2:30	Finished book for tonight's book group
		3 - 4:30	Dental cleanings for David and me
		5 - 5:30	Scanned newspaper
		5:30 - 7:00	Prepared dinner, ate, cleaned up
		7:30 - 9:30	Good book group discussion; Should write characters' names, etc. next book so easier to participate
		10 - 11:30	Finished newspaper; watched TV late news

ENDURANCE is the ability to focus attention on what you want for as long as you want. Training strengthens it. Being able to focus your attention requires you to concentrate, overcome interference, be more observant, listen better, follow directions, and develop self-discipline. Resistance Training exercises build needed stamina.

ORGANIZATION is the process by which data are implanted and retained. The brain associates fresh input with information already stored or records it as new data. *MFW* exercises promote conscious association-making ability. Language is the primary form through which linking occurs.

Make your dictionary your new best friend. When you are not sure of a word, look it up. Language resists the onslaught of years, is reinforced by exercise and is integral to retention.

However, not everything stored in your brain gets there in a logical, organized, left-brain fashion. Your out-of-the-box right brain also plays a major role. It intuits and creates a personal file of original associations, especially as visual images, which promote insight and comprehension, support creativity and reinforce memory.

You have often heard that one picture is worth a thousand words. Nowhere is this truer than with respect to memory. Mental images, the pictures you form in your mind's eye, are retained and recalled better than words; therefore, exercise to strengthen your visualizing skills. Mental Aerobics and Visualization work target language and linkage.

FLEXIBILITY is tied closely to perception and organization. How do you see things? What associations do you make? Are you stuck in a rut, or are you capable of seeing things in a new light, of doing things in a different way? Can you see both sides of an issue? Can you understand another's point of view - even if you don't agree?

Strengthening muscles to keep your brain supple will make you less rigid and increase your tolerance and capacity for open mindedness. Flexibility increases your potential to cope effectively with new situations in your daily life, frees thinking, allows new ideas to percolate, and generates perceptions others may not have had. Another name for these dynamics is creativity. Mental Gymnastic exercises encourage these kinds of activities.

COORDINATION is heavy work. Input gets processed. Associations are integrated. Insights occur. Solutions are sought. Ideas develop. It's the seat of reasoning and problem solving. Sprints and Weight Lifting show results in this arena.

CONSCIOUS RECALL is the principle difficulty for people past 50 years of age. Much of the material we struggle to evoke is not forgotten; therefore, it is important to learn how to find and extract it more easily. Spatial clues provide orientation, a three-dimensional mental image, which facilitates locating desired material. Temporal clues consist of mentally created before/after images; it is more difficult to see oneself in time than space. These clues are used to recruit associations linked to sought after content.

Mnemonic devices are excellent memory aids, as are Stretching exercises which require expansive mental maneuvers. Both techniques force you to locate and retrieve information.

You've been using mental muscles, unconsciously, naturally all your life - in school, on the job, socially. Chances are, however, you're no longer a student, you might be retired, and you may not get around much any more. That's why, like the biceps, quads and abs you exercise in physical workouts, you need to exercise your brain's muscles in *Mental Fitness Workouts*.

MENTAL FUNCTIONS

Strengthening your mental muscles adds to your comprehensive cognitive capabilities. The brain performs functions we take for granted at our own peril. Language, Logic, Spatial Orientation, Creativity, and Memory are just a few that depend on the muscles identified above.

❖ Language permits effective communication, i.e., the message you send is the message received.
❖ Logic enables you to recognize fallacies in thinking - yours and other's. It entails reasoning and sound judgment.
❖ Spatial Orientation enhances your mind's eye. Not only does it help you to get your bearings and see the whole picture, it facilitates mental flexibility.

❖ Creativity takes many forms. In addition to the fine, performing and creative arts, there's gardening, crafts, cooking, carpentry, and innovative problem solving.

❖ Memory, the function about which most people grow most anxious, gives you your historic sense of self and the world in which you live and allows you to profit from your experience. How does memory relate to mental muscles? Mental muscles buttress the foundation that supports memory.

Memory is *not* a one-step, all-or-nothing phenomenon; it is a complicated process, still not fully understood. However, memory's very complexity affords you opportunities to intercede at different stages in the operation with a variety of methods designed to improve, strengthen and train it.

Age Smart is a mental fitness training program that targets the muscles memory depends on for support. Memory, remember, is a sensitive, complex mechanism. It varies directly with motivation, emotion and fatigue. The more important the content and the stronger the emotion - good or bad - the stronger the memory. The more tired you are, the less well you remember. Memory also relies heavily on perception, concentration, and association, some of the muscles you are going to bulk up.

AGE SMART

MENTAL FITNESS WORKOUT
#2

RELAXATION WARM-UP
Follow the directions on Page 11.

MENTAL CALISTHENICS

C 2a	Think of a country beginning with	A
	Think of an animal beginning with	G
	Think of a fruit ending with	E
	Think of a color beginning with	S
	Think of a tree ending with	M
	Think of a car ending with	A
	Think of a dog beginning with	R
	Think of an article of clothing ending with	T

C 2b Count aloud to 100 as quickly as you can, going up by 5 and down by 3. Start at 5:

5-2, 7-4, 9-6 ...98-103, 100.

Repeat this mini-mental-massage whenever you have time with numbers you choose.

SENSORY DRILLS

A 2 Listen for the following sounds. Keep a list in your MFJ of those you hear. The first time you do this exercise, try to hear the indicated sounds within one hour. Thereafter, make the exercise more rigorous each time you do it by decreasing the time allowed and/or increasing the number of sounds you listen for.

√	√√		√√√	
Dog	Dog	Bell	Dog	Airplane
Cat	Cat	Whistle	Cat	Helicopter
Bird	Bird	Siren	Bird	Train
Bell	Thud	Squeak	Thud	Automobile
			Bell	Motorcycle
			Whistle	Wind
			Siren	Thunder
			Squeak	Lightning

TA 2 Ask someone to prepare a meal for you. Try to identify the food on your plate by taste only. If possible, eat while you are blind folded.

How successful were you? Which foods were easy to identify? Which difficult?

What did you do to help yourself identify the tastes, especially the less obvious ones? Which other sense might have given you a clue? Respond to these questions in your MFJ.

ISOMETRICS

I 2 Look at the designs in the box below for 10 seconds. Then cover them and continue reading directions.

Look at the box below and in less than 15 seconds, identify the design that did not appear in the first box. Write the corresponding number in your MJF.

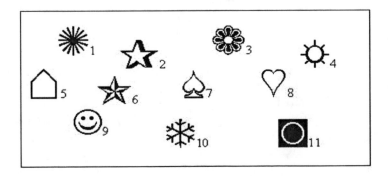

VISUALIZATION

Vz 2 Visualize and draw your computer keyboard. Draw it again as you look at it. Wait a day or two, and draw it from memory. Do this exercise with other familiar objects - the car dashboard, your radio alarm clock, a telephone pad - to sharpen your powers of observation and get you to habitually PAY ATTENTION.

SPRINTS

Sp 2 Name as many countries as you can in South America in one minute.

MENTAL GYMNASTICS

MG 2 Read a newspaper paragraph upside down. Record the time it takes in your MFJ. Extend your upside-down reading every day until you can do it for five minutes. You will be creating new neural connections and patterns. This is how you grow your brain and make it stronger.

RESISTANCE TRAINING

RT 2 Take some printed material you can mark up, e.g., a newspaper article, a page from an old magazine. Cross out every "n" as quickly as you can on half the page. Estimate how many n_s there were. Repeat the exercise to see if you missed any. Write the number of estimated n_s and the actual number of n_s in your MFJ. You can repeat this exercise with any letter.

MENTAL AEROBICS

MA 2 Develop your logic. Build your capacity to see and sort by commonalities. In your MJF, arrange the following lists of words in categories. Give a title to each category, and explain your choice of title.

√ Agenda, Tulips, Instructor, Notepad, Gladiolas, Lawyer, File, Rose, Pharmacist, Iris, Doctor, Minutes

√√ Architect, Dog, Hammer, Wine, Tiger, Electrician, Martini, Pliers, Elephant, Water, Nurse, Wrench, Squirrel, Photographer, Screw Driver, Lemonade

√√√ Violin, Chair, Necklace, Checkers, Tennis, Footstool, Bridge, Ring, Couch, Accordion, Brooch, Bed, Football, Piano, Chess, Bracelet, Table, Flute, Basketball, Backgammon, Guitar, Tiara, Credenza, Gymnastics

WEIGHT LIFTING

WL 2 Copy these two multiplication examples into your MFJ. Study them for 15 seconds. Then fill in the missing numbers as quickly as you can.

```
      7 ∎ 4              6 3 ∎
   x  1 ∎           x  4 ∎ 3
   1 ∎ 2 ∎            1 9 0 ∎
   ∎ ∎ 4              3 ∎ 7 ∎
   ∎ ∎ 6 ∎          2 ∎ ∎ 6
                    ∎ 8 7 2 0 ∎
```

STRETCHING

St 2 Shake up your brain's grooved patterns. Take a different route to a store, the movies, any destination. It may be less efficient, but you'll have to think about where you're going and how to get there. Too often you're on "automatic pilot."

CONSCIOUS RECALL

CR 2 In your MFJ, describe in full detail what you were wearing yesterday morning. If you changed clothes during the day or evening, describe your new garb, too.

COOL DOWN

Look at the characteristics of Mentally Fit People on Page 18. In your MFJ, list those you consider to be your personal Mental Fitness Strengths. In another column, indicate areas you think Need Improvement. Begin to recognize these behaviors in yourself and others, and try to work on those you want to upgrade.

Evaluate your behavior, progress and ability to recognize Mental Fitness characteristics in others. Keep an

anecdotal record of your efforts and the results in your
MFJ.

Explain what you are trying to do to someone you
trust, and ask for his/her input. It's always wise to vali-
date your subjective impressions with another's (hopefully)
more objective data.

Grow old as slowly as possible.

Anonymous

3

AGE HAPPY

Tolstoy may have said happy families are all alike, but everyone experiences happiness differently, in different forms, at different levels. There's waking up to a sunny day, passing a tough exam, hearing baby's first words, having fun at a party, falling in love, listening to great music.

We say we're "happy" when we feel enjoyment, relief, pleasure, and accomplishment. Happiness varies with events, culture and genes. Happiness, also, is more than just not being unhappy.

When a positive event happens, the body sends a message to the brain. "Happy" signals increase the pulse rate and skin temperature and make the muscles relax. See how happy you feel the next time your muscles are tense or you have goose bumps.

Every feeling, including happiness, depends on the brain and body exchanging signals. We experience the emotional side of happiness as feelings of joy and delight. Satisfaction is the name we give to the cognitive dimension.

HOW HAPPY ARE YOU?

Some of the more than 100 billion synapses in our brain - where nerve impulses are transmitted among nerve cells - form a happiness circuit. In other words, we're programmed for positive feelings.

At the same time, research indicates we are born with a genetically set "happiness-level range" within which we usually function. The level may rocket up or plummet down, depending upon events, but the changes are not permanent.

Over time, we resume living within our set range. Within a year, for example, both lottery winners and paralyzed accident victims find themselves approximately back in their base moods. Nature seems to have designed us to adjust to both positive and negative events so we remain productive and continue to contribute as best we can.

But genes are not destiny. They affect how you're inclined to respond to experiences; they do not determine your response. Your brain does that.

Slightly more than half of the American respondents to a World Values Survey, carried out four times since 1981, indicated they were "Quite Happy."

How would you describe yourself? Take into account how you usually feel, how you see yourself compared to many people you know and how you would like to be.

Your Happiness Coefficient

1	2	3	4	5
Not Very Happy				Very Happy

On the scale above, select the Happiness Coefficient that best describes you, and enter the number in your MFJ. Do you think others see you the same way? It would be interesting to ask the people you compared yourself to how they see you. You might find it informative to clarify any discrepancies between you-as-you-see-yourself, you-as-others-see-you and you-as-you-would-like-to-be.

WHAT MAKES US HAPPY?

When asked what makes them happy, most respondents put "family and friends" first and include the events usually enjoyed with them - dining, drinking, recreation, and sex.

1. Social Interaction

2. Goal Attainment

3. Leisure Activities

Note if you will, how evolution has seen to it that activities which contribute to preserving our species make us happy. We eat because Nature has made hunger unpleasant. Babies' natural smiles encourage ecstatic adults to take care of them.

Not only is Social Interaction *numero uno* on the source of happiness scale, it was cited above as a <u>basic</u> <u>component</u> <u>of</u> <u>successful</u> <u>aging</u>, as important as "resistance to disease" and "physical and mental fitness." We need other people to help us survive, and we need them to help us age well. Independence is great - as long as you have a strong support group behind you.

The two other main sources of happiness people cite are 1) attaining goals and 2) leisure activities. Accomplishments, both mental and physical, generate a powerful reward - the intrinsic satisfaction you get from successfully applying your skills. When goal pursuits and leisure activities are done in the company of others, they confer added important social benefits.

Music, other arts and religion are considered pleasures of the mind. They also can evoke deep emotion.

IT'S GOOD TO BE HAPPY

The benefits of happiness are manifold. Happy people tend to enjoy numerous and rewarding social relationships, a significant determinant of successful aging. Happy people are predisposed to accentuate the positive and have a warm, open, friendly style. Both their outlook and manner appeal to others. Think of yourself. Don't you prefer the company of smiling faces to sour pusses?

In addition, there is a strong correlation between happiness and good health. Research reported in 2001 in the *Journal of Personality and Social Psychology* indicates Happy people live longer. Good moods elevate the immune system, another manifestation of the mind/body connection, and help to guard against illness.

Positive feelings counteract stress. Fear, depression and tension activate stress hormones, which unfortunately reduce resistance to illness and are associated with heart problems and stroke. While stress hormones have not been shown to cause cancer, recent research reported in the journal *Cancer Research* suggests they may increase a tumor's growth rate and hasten metastasis.

Happiness increases mental productivity. It stimulates the growth of nerve connections. They make us smarter, more creative and cooperative as well as better, quicker problem solvers.

Happy people have greater self-esteem, autonomy, optimism, and sense of purpose. In other words, Happiness not only may lengthen your life, it adds significantly to the quality of it.

WHO'S HAPPY?

Several personality traits are associated with happiness. Extroverts demonstrate behaviors that correlate highly with happiness. They tend to be socially engaged, involved in positive activities and enjoy a sense of well-being. They're out there living, giving it their all.

Of course, there are happy introverts, but not as many. Introverts derive their happiness from quieter, more solitary sources.

Is your glass half full or half empty? Optimism and pessimism are traits that significantly affect happiness levels. According to Martin Seligman, Ph.D., the father of Positive Psychology, the way we react to negative events significantly affects our subjective estimates of happiness.

Optimists see negative events as temporary setbacks, specific to an incident and caused by circumstances or bad luck. Pessimists, on the other hand, see them as pervasive, permanent and personal, i.e., everything always goes wrong, it's their fault and there's nothing they can do to change it. Optimists explain negative events the way pessimists do positive events and *vice versa.*

Because they believe they can affect what happens, optimists take steps to develop better health habits, a more energetic immune system, and a more active, stronger social support system. The result, as noted, is they live longer. Optimists also experience less negativity as a result of their good health. Unpleasing life events have a high positive correlation with illness.

Moreover, action-prone positive thinkers make an effort to avoid or prevent what they don't want to happen and respond assertively to problems. Pessimists tend to be passive (Nothing I do makes a difference.) and don't act to ward off unpleasantness. Their anxiety and worry obstruct positive life events and invite negative ones.

Learned helplessness is an unfortunate corollary of pessimism. If you believe nothing you do will improve matters, you give up and don't exercise whatever power you do have. That may be one reason optimists are healthier than pessimists. The latter, thinking nothing they do makes a difference, may not see doctors when they should, take the medications they need, eat nutritionally, exercise, or socialize enough.

Your mind set affects your immune system. Your brain and immune system are connected by neurotransmitters, chemical messengers. When you are depressed, and pessimists are depressed more often than optimists, your immune system hunkers down in direct correlation, i.e., the greater your depression, the lower your immune system.

This helps to explain why major changes that may have negative aspects - retirement, relocation, an altered relationship, the illness or death of a loved one - can seriously impair health. Depressed immune systems are not as protective as robust ones. For example, widowers are more likely to die within six months of a spouse's death than at other times. If a spouse dies, friends and relatives should prompt the survivor to have a complete health exam not too long after the sad event. A weakened defense system and/or increased stress hormones could prove dangerous to the griever's health.

Nevertheless, there are occasions when it is wise to adopt a pessimist's approach. Because they anticipate negativity, pessimists analyze situations more thoroughly, cautiously and realistically. After all, we are programmed to be alert to threats to our safety and well-being. Therefore, in high-risk situations, it's safer to be a bit of a pessimist.

I WANT TO BE HAPPY

Are you fated by genetically predisposed personality traits to a predetermined level of happiness? Fortunately, no. You have the ability to stack the Happiness odds in your favor through activity, social engagement, financial planning, and by working on behalf of something you value.

Believe it or not, the fastest, most direct natural way to a more positive mood is through physical exercise. The activity releases endorphins, which generate feelings of euphoria, power and control. That's why physical exercise is often prescribed instead of medicine for depression.

Rousseau said, "For the mind's sake, it's necessary to exercise the body." And if you exercise with others, you add the positive effects of socialization.

The next quickest drug-free way to a good mood is through music. It soothes the savage breast.

Since the company of others is the major source of good moods for most people, try to stay socially engaged. Join groups, take classes. Positive interpersonal relationships, more than anything else, keep us Happy.

They are more important than money, work, home, or leisure activities.

The relationship between happiness and income is greater at the lower end of the economic scale. Once a survival safety level has been attained, finances do not significantly contribute to happiness. Although average incomes have more than doubled in western society, people are no happier than they were 50 years ago.

Actually, there's been an increase in depression. It seems the more we have, the more we want. Income appears to have less effect on well-being than social relationships, having a purpose in life and for those still employed, rewarding work.

Nevertheless, financial security affects contentedness. Money worries can interfere with Happiness. Longevity may bring fear of outliving income or incurring huge medical and/or nursing home costs. It is incumbent upon all, regardless of health or income, to learn about protecting their own or a loved one's tangible assets, pensions, savings, transfers, and gifts. Everyone should become informed about long term care insurance, Medicare and Medicaid, and pertinent legal rights, requirements and responsibilities.

These matters are complicated. If you can afford it, talk to a lawyer experienced in this field. Otherwise, Elder Services provides valuable information and counseling with respect to these issues. Knowing your affairs are settled as much to your advantage as possible brings relief, a welcome source of happiness.

Goals give meaning to life. Working on behalf of something outside yourself and bigger than yourself affords satisfaction, self-esteem and purpose, bottom-line determinants of Happiness. In his book *Man's Search for Meaning*, holocaust survivor Victor Frankl stresses the life affirming value of pursuing freely chosen, realistic, attainable goals.

Striving for more than is realistically possible can generate depression, but so does living without purpose.

There are enough causes and organizations to work for to enable you to engage in activities that afford a sense of well-being, personal agency, social contact, an opportunity to use preferred skills, involvement in community, a sense of control over one's life, and self-esteem. These positive feelings add up to authentic Happiness.

CHASING THE BLUES AWAY

What happens, though, if negative thoughts persist? Battle them; refute them. Your power to deliberately change your thoughts and the feelings they generate gives you power over sadness and depression.

Albert Ellis, considered by many to be the grandfather of cognitive therapy, postulated behavioral ABC's. A, there's a stimulus; B, the brain forms a belief - it's good for me, bad for me; C is the consequence - a feeling, a response.

As you can see, *thinking precedes feeling.* Therefore, to change your feelings about something, you need to change the way you think about it. You are an idiosyncratic physical, mental and emotional system. Change one part, e.g., your beliefs about something, and you impact the system, including your feelings and behavior.

How truly important is some of what bothers you? There is *always* someone who is smarter, does things differently from you, can do them better, and has more than you. Yes, there are real problems, but if you want to be Happy, try to be less judgmental and opt for a positive attitude.

Your brain has the power to enable you to choose Happiness, sincerity and authenticity. Your inner satisfaction will reward your choices.

We respond and function according to messages we send ourselves. If you are discontented, change the messages you send yourself. Your beliefs about the world determine the world you see. Hamlet said it a long time ago, "For there is nothing good nor bad, but thinking makes it so."

When pessimistic thoughts arise, confront and disprove them. Argue, dispute, test them against what actually occurs. What evidence supports them? What may be alternative explanations? Somewhere, sometime, you know you did something right. Think about that!

When ideas about how terrible something or someone is surface, tell yourself "Stop." Start sending positive thoughts. Make yourself remember a pleasant experience.

Some people pinch themselves, bite their tongue, snap a rubber band against their wrist to stop unpleasant thoughts and change the message. It takes practice, but there are methods to use to help you change the way you think.

If you keep doing/thinking the same thing and it's not getting you where or how you want to be, doesn't it make sense to change? Yes, you can. Believing you can change permits it to happen. Remember, whether you think you can or can't do something, you're right.

Your brain is the most flexible system you have. No other organ has the same capacity for change. It's what enables you to change your mind and opinions, like foods you used to hate, develop new hobbies, make new friends, learn to do Sudoku- the list is endless. Your brain likes to learn new things and be challenged. That's how it grows, stays sharp and keeps you cognitively competent.

Take advantage of this flexibility. Try the different and new. Novelty pleases the brain. Learn to enjoy the unexpected. Pleasant surprises are one of the strongest sources of pleasure. Remember how delighted you were when you stumbled upon a rather unprepossessing restaurant in a little out-of-the-way town and were served a delicious dinner? Or stayed at a charming, inexpensive B & B not listed in the tour books?

Focus on an interest - the more you know about a subject, the more interesting, rewarding, and enjoyable it becomes. Take up gardening, photography or learn about contemporary art. Get politically involved. Study a foreign language. Many who didn't grow up with computers and felt threatened when PCs first appeared, now surf the net with aplomb (and Google).

Engaging in activities you like engenders good spirits. When you're happy, you're more active. The more active you are.... It's a good cycle to ride.

Optimism can be learned. The way you look at the world - your perceptions and interpretations - affects the way you feel. But you do not have to be held hostage by your belief system. It is possible to change and send yourself more positive, Happiness-producing messages.

You need to remind yourself to generate social capital. Invest it in enjoyable activities that enable you to be involved with people, use the skills you like and work on behalf of ideas, causes and organizations you support.

A wise person once said people keep busy looking for Happiness, but they are happiest keeping busy.

AGE SMART

MENTAL FITNESS WORKOUT
 # 3

RELAXATION WARM-UP
Follow the directions on Page 11.

MENTAL CALISTHENICS
C 3a Say as many words as you can in 15 seconds that begin with each of your initials. This is a good exercise to do whenever you have some spare time. Use the initials of friends, family and famous people.

C 3b Count aloud as quickly as possible from 1 to 100, saying only numbers that contain the figure 3 or 8.

SENSORY DRILLS

O 3 In a restaurant, at home, in the street, try to identify foods not in your line of sight by their odor. In your MFJ, list the ones you identify correctly. Describe any memories that may be evoked.

The sense of smell is a powerful memory clue because the olfactory nerve goes directly into the brain. Unfortunately, the nerve may become less sensitive with age, so do this exercise whenever the opportunity arises.

TO 3 Open a drawer. Without looking, feel and identify the objects in the drawer. List the ones you correctly identify in your MJF.

ISOMETRICS

I 3 First look carefully at the figure below for 10 seconds. Then cover it. In 15 seconds, see if you can tell how many different kinds of arrows there are and how they are arranged. Write the answer in your MFJ.

VISUALIZATION

Vz 3 Visualize a perfect gift for each member of your family and/or close friends. Truly <u>see</u> it, as opposed to just thinking of it, and describe it in detail in your MFJ. Explain your choices.

SPRINT

Sp 3 Name $\sqrt{8}$, $\sqrt{\sqrt{}}$12, $\sqrt{\sqrt{\sqrt{}}}$15 objects used in kitchens.

MENTAL GYMNASTICS

MG 3 SCRAMBLED COUNTRIES: Match the groups of letters correctly to spell the names of 10 countries, each containing six letters. The first group of two letters is in column one. The next two letters are in column two, and the last two, in column three. A sample has been underlined and entered on the first line.
Write the other country names in your MFJ.

1	2	3	Country
CA	AZ	AY	CANADA
PO	XI	ND	
NO	RK	US	
CY	RW	EN	
ME	*NA*	EL	
TU	PR	CE	
BR	LA	CO	
SW	RA	EY	
IS	AN	*DA*	
FR	ED	IL	

RESISTANCE TRAINING

RT 3 Copy and complete the following grid in your MFJ. Enter a word for each subject listed on the left under each letter in SMART.

	S	M	A	R	T
Animals					
Cities					
Colors					
Authors					
Flowers					
Foods					

MENTAL AEROBICS

MA 3 Correctly read aloud at sight the following passages in which each word is spelled backwards. Then write the correctly spelled sentences in your MFJ.

√ gnieB yleritne tsenoh htiw fleseno si a doog
esicrexe – *dmumgiS duerF*

erehT si on etutitsbus rof drah krow – *samohT nosidE*

√√ tuB ni ecneics eht tiderc seog ot eht nam ohw
secnivnoc eht dlrow, ton ot eht nam ot mohw
eht aedi tsrif scrucco – *riS sicnarF niwraD*

ehT tsehgih dna tseb mrof fo ycneiciffe si eht
suoenatnops noitarepooc fo a eerf elpoep
– *wordooW nosliW*

√√√ roF ccnatsni, ereht si eht dnik fo ssensuoires
esohw kramedart si hsiugna, ytleurc,
tnemegnared – *nasuS gatnoS*

nredoM raw si os evisnepxe taht ew leef edart ot
eb a retteb euneva ot rednulp.... gniwohS s'raw
ytilanoitarri dna rorroh si fo on tceffe nopu mih.
ehT srorroh ekam eht noitanicsaf – *mailliW
semaJ*

tI si yrev tluciffid os tluciffid taht ti syawla sah
neeb tluciffid tub neve erom tluciffid won ot
wonk tahw si eht noitaler fo namuh erutan ot
eht namuh dnim esuaceb eno sah ot wonk tahw
si eht noitaler fo eht tca fo noitaerc ot eht
tcejbus eht rotaerc sesu ot etaerc taht gniht
– *edurtreG nietS*

WEIGHT LIFTING

WL 3 In your MFJ, write the word that can be made with the letters at the intersections of the words below.

```
            C O M P L E T E
                L
                E
        A P A R T
                S           C
                E N V E L O P E S
                        O       U
                  A C C U S E   P
                  S     D       P O W E R
                  K             L
                                Y
```

STRETCHING

St 3 Think of something you would like to see changed: policies, programs, behavior, traffic patterns, pet peeves. Imagine ways to change it and write about it in your MFJ.

Expand your brain. Improvise. Don't worry about practicality or cost. You might even come up with a good idea.

CONSCIOUS RECALL

CR 3 Write the names of as many places as come to mind in one minute for √ the letter P, √√ the letters USA and √√√ the letters in THANKS.

COOL DOWN

Carefully consider the suggestions offered above for increasing your level of Happiness. In your MFJ, make note of those that appeal to you. Describe how you could make them work for you.

In your log, note times and situations in which you felt Happy or not as Happy as you would have liked. Explain why you felt as you did. Where appropriate, relate what might have made you Happier.

Think of where, when and how you have the power to elevate your Happiness level. Describe what you could do to raise it.

It's never too late to dream a new dream.
Anonymous

OVERCOMING OBSTACLES

The way you handle aging is shaped in large measure by your expectations. They, in turn, are generated by your beliefs, many of which are grounded in myth. Myths cause and exaggerate fears. To accept these myths is self-defeating. Believing in them makes you think there is nothing you can do to affect how you age; therefore, you don't do all you can and should do to age well. It's a form of self-defeating learned helplessness. These myths take away the motivation to age pro-actively. They prevent you from exercising control and power over the way you live longer.

CORRECT FOR DISTORTION

To develop a more accurate understanding of aging and more realistic expectations, let's revisit some popular myths about aging and correct for distortion. These myths create a lot of baggage you can well do without.

MYTH # 1 — *We're not mentally sharp as we get older because we lose all those brain cells.*

The effects of aging on the brain are minimal in terms of aging well. You are born with billions of nerve cells that form learning and memory connections (synapses) throughout life. Yes, some brain cells do die, but new ones grow and synapses are generated and develop complexity regardless of age. They are always there for you.

In reality, most of us use less than 80 percent of our brain cells. OK, you say, then why are there so many? Biologists hypothesize that millions of nerve cells are like subs sitting on the bench, waiting for the coach to put them into the game should the team need help.

Indeed, you have more than enough nerve cells in your brain to last a lifetime, with a sufficient majority in reserve should they be needed to take over in the case of injuries or illness. This phenomenon is called the brain's built-in *plasticity.*

If necessary, reserve nerve cells can be trained to take over the jobs of damaged or dead neurons. This is called functional plasticity and is what happens, for example, when a stroke survivor learns to walk or talk again.

Nerve cells' structural plasticity is especially important for people who want to *Age Smart.* Think of a nerve cell as a plant with a long tap root (the axon) at one end and many branching stems (dendrites) at the other.

NEURON

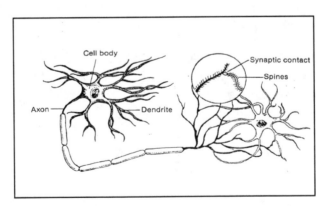

A nerve cell receives electrochemical impulses from other neurons through its axon and forwards the message impulses to more neurons through connections formed by its dendrites. Whenever you have a new experience, every time you learn something, stimulated nerve cells sprout new dendrites, thus increasing their transmission capability and physically restructuring your brain.

These modifications affect your beliefs, feelings, moods, and actions. Brain change affects who you are, how you feel, what you think, and helps you cope throughout life. Thus, even the aging mind has the capacity to grow, learn and change.

Scientists are excited by research demonstrating the brain's remarkable ability to develop and adapt. Evidence of their belief in the brain's plasticity can be seen in recent studies involving 10-year stroke survivors. Subjects' brains are being electronically stimulated to restore movement many years after the trauma.

Mental exercises strengthen your brain by stimulating new synapses and reinforcing existing ones. They capitalize on the brain's plasticity, capacity and ability to grow the mind.

The body needs exercise to build and maintain physical muscles; the brain needs exercise to build and maintain mental muscles. *Use it or lose it* applies to both mind and body.

MYTH # 2   *You can't teach an old dog new tricks.*

The latest research confirms your brain's ability to form new synapses, absorb new data and retain fundamentals throughout life. As you age, for example, your verbal intelligence doesn't decline. You don't "forget" how to write, how to speak, how to read.

In fact, these skills can increase. An experimental group of people 65 and older was given five hours of training in spatial orientation and reasoning skills. Two thirds of the group showed mental improvement. Six months later, a significant number still tested stronger.

The results of a recent NIA funded study strongly support these findings. A significant number of more than 2800 healthy, independent adults, also 65 and older, showed less decline five years after training in memory, reasoning and processing than did the untrained control group.

Mental activity keeps the brain in top condition. Cogitating is to the brain what movement is to the body. When confronted by a problem, whether it's how to get out of the path of a speeding car, what investment to make or book to read, the brain shifts into gear.

It perceives (something is happening), evaluates (it's good/bad for me), associates (this relates to...), sorts (it belongs in this category), remembers (this has/has not happened to me before), analyzes (it means...), compares (it is the same/different), thinks (my options are...), and decides (I shall do...). Sometimes the whole process takes less than a split second; sometimes, hours of careful deliberation or days of indecision. No matter.

While the process is going on, neurotransmitters zip through synapses, capillaries expand and blood flow increases bringing more oxygen in, taking carbon dioxide out. This mental activity is what keeps your brain in shape longer, makes a big difference in the way you function and gives you the opportunity to affect the way you age. This is why it is so important to exercise your brain.

What may decline, however, is the speed at which you recall what you're trying to remember and some ability to process information. But that's OK. You don't run the mile as fast as you used to, either.

Given time, older people do as well as younger people on tests of cognitive ability. Groping for words is a fairly common feature as people age. It can be embarrassing and frustrating, but it is not really serious. There's a big difference between not remembering the name of a movie you saw last year or even last night, forgetting the name of an old school friend and not knowing your own name.

Give yourself time. That word or name you know so well that it's on the tip of your tongue will surface. It is not forgotten, it's not lost; sometimes, it just takes a little longer to find it.

The secret of successful aging is to choose the right parents.

Only about 30-40 percent of the characteristics of aging can be attributed to heredity. Moreover, the role genes play grows less important with increasing age. Life style choices are more likely to cause the unpleasant physical and mental conditions people blame on aging.

Over eating, poor nutrition, smoking, too much alcohol, lack of regular physical and mental exercise, taking an array of uncoordinated medications, and insufficient social contact can cause more problems than the aging process itself. Even cognitive depreciation can be generated by unwise behavior.

Behavioral factors, however, are not diseases and are subject to your control. Not only may some unpleasant physical and mental conditions be preventable, they might even be reversible. Again, it's your call. You can change your life style.

LIFE STYLE PROFILE

The following is a list of unhealthy life style behaviors. How many are descriptive of the way you live?

UNHEALTHY LIFE STYLE FACTORS

- Smoking
- Poor Nutrition
    Too Much Food
    Unhealthy Food
- Too Much Alcohol
- Not Enough Exercise
    Physical
    Mental
- Unmonitored Medications
- Insufficient Social Interaction

What is your life style profile? Be honest. How closely do you resemble the unhealthy descriptors cited below? Copy the list into your MFJ and rate yourself on each according to the scale shown. Remember, the higher the number, the healthier the behavior.

MY LIFE STYLE PROFILE

1	5	10
Like Me		Unlike Me

DESCRIPTOR	SCORE
Smoker	
Pig Out	
Fast Food Fanatic	
Set'em Up Joe	
Couch Potato	
Mental Laggard	
Medication Mess	
Shut-In	
Total LSP _____	

Enter your total Life Style Profile score in your MFJ. A perfect LSP is 80. How satisfied are you with yours? Where do you see room for improvement?

In your MFJ, note the area/s you plan to work on.

THE MIND/BODY CONNECTION

Let's look more closely at how behavior, health and fitness are entwined and the tight relationship between mental activity and the body. As scientists better understand the fit, the more they appreciate and respect it. The connection is seamless, and you are about as conscious of it as you are of breathing. But you know about it experientially.

When you are on an emotional high, all's well, and you feel fine. Nothing hurts. But when you're stressed or depressed, everything is too much; you have no energy. Furthermore, when you are sick, it's not unusual to feel irritable, sluggish, blue. Remember how down you were and how hard it was to concentrate on anything last time you had the flu?

Physical fitness contributes to mental fitness primarily through improved circulation. We know improved circulation benefits the heart. But the mind? Absolutely. Improved circulation increases the blood flow to the brain. This supplies more of the nutrients (glucose, the brain's food), chemicals (neurotransmitters) and elements (especially oxygen) the brain needs to perform well.

The mind-body connection is a two-way street. Examples of how the mind directly affects the body include emotions, sex, visualization, and biofeedback. Strong proof of the mind's effect on the body is the placebo effect, a somatic result caused solely by belief in the treatment.

EMOTIONS express themselves physically. People who are nervous perspire, feel "butterflies" in their stomach, frequently clear their throat, and frequent the restroom. When fearful, they shiver with fright and feel their heart leap into their throat, their stomach drop, the hairs on their arms stand on end, or their legs grow so weak they can't stand. All are physical reactions generated by the mind.

SEX is a prime example of mind over matter. Most men and women are familiar with the intimate tie between erotic thoughts, mental images and bodily responses. Many sex therapists maintain more people have sex problems in their heads than their bodies. Pornography sells well for good reason.

VISUALIZATION is another demonstration of the mind's effect on the body. Beginning golfers and tennis players, for example, are taught to "see" themselves swinging the club or stroking the ball to groove the motion so their mind can help their body remember.

An anecdote is told about Jean Claude Killy, the great skier. He had to practice for his next race; the problem was he had broken a leg during the preceding one. He watched movies, memorized the new route and visualized the slope, the course, the gates, and himself skiing down the mountain.

Records of his heart rate and muscle contractions as he sat in his chair, leg in cast, show his body responded to the mental images as though he were actually skiing. The body can't tell it is only a mind movie. The body thinks it's the real thing and responds accordingly. The body does what the mind tells it.

If you still want proof, try the following experiment. First read the directions through to the end.

"Do this with your eyes closed. Relax and visualize a bright, shiny yellow lemon on a counter top; see yourself pick it up, look at it, handle it slowly, sniff it, feel the texture of the skin; take the sharp knife lying next to it and cut the lemon in quarters; inhale the fragrance of the fresh, juicy lemon; see the droplets of juice on the cut surface; pick up one piece of the lemon; hold it close to your nose and smell it; finally, open your mouth, put the lemon on your tongue, and suck the juice." If you did this without salivating, you're one of few.

Job seekers are counseled to visualize themselves being interviewed, to imagine the office, the interviewer, themselves dressed appropriately, speaking well, making a good impression, carrying it off as they would like it to go. Rehearsing a successful interview in their mind's eye makes them less nervous on the big day. Most of us mentally rehearse big moments. The body gets the message, "Been there, done that; don't have to be so nervous and afraid."

BIO-FEEDBACK is the mind/body connection in action. More than 20 years ago, Dr. Herbert Benson wrote about the "relaxation response." He discussed the scientific verification of the mind's ability to generate physiological effects. Evidence shows the relaxation response can help to reduce stress-related heart attacks and strokes. Many people meditate to lower their blood pressure.

THE PLACEBO EFFECT fascinates and amazes doctors. Through the 1940s, much prescribed medicine relied on the placebo effect, a physiological result caused only by the patient's faith in a medication or process. In other words, a biological change occurs because the patient, not knowing the treatment is fake, strongly believes in its effectiveness. Today, even though pharmacology is far more advanced, the interest in placebos remains because of their amazing results: Placebos have been shown to be 50-60 percent as effective as aspirin or codeine for pain relief.

Placebos are a powerful demonstration of mind over matter. The evidence is remarkable. In a group of balding men whose heads were treated with a placebo, 42 percent actually grew hair. A group of South American children with severe asthma increased their lung performance by a third from inhaling a placebo. In Japan, a group of people highly allergic to poison ivy developed a real rash from touching what they thought were poison ivy leaves. Two years after an arthroscopic surgery experiment in Texas, the group that received the placebo treatment reported the same amount of relief from pain and swelling as the patients who were actually operated on.

How does this phenomenon work? The explanation, "Expectancy Theory," emanates from a branch of cognitive neuropsychology. According to doctors in the field, "If you expect to get better, you will." The mind sets up a self-fulfilling prophecy. Take it a step further. Expect to age well. Adopt a positive outlook, a beneficent mental set. The body achieves what the mind believes.

THE M/B CONNECTION: MAKE IT WORK FOR YOU

Your mind controls your body. Learn to use the connection to your advantage. Let's review why it is important to keep this interrelated system in good repair. The benefits of mental and physical fitness include the ability to cope more effectively, heal faster, feel good about yourself, perform better, and keep the brain healthy.

When you are mentally and physically fit, you function more effectively and are able to overcome obstacles more effectively. You feel and act sharp.

You heal better, too. A recent study in the *Journals of Gerontology* noted wounds on healthy adults who exercised, healed significantly faster than on non-exercisers in the control group.

Physically and mentally fit people feel good about themselves and have a positive attitude. They have greater self-confidence, are not afraid to meet and talk to people, engage in activities, and remain involved in life.

The benefits can be seen on an interpersonal level. Other people usually prefer the company of men and women who have a positive attitude; they're more fun to be with. And as noted above, social interaction contributes significantly to aging well.

Furthermore, research has shown that positive self-regard benefits the brain chemically. Data show men and women with high self-esteem generate a lower level of free radicals, the stress hormones that destroy brain cells connected to memory, and cortisol, a stress-related hormone that decreases the immune system. This is a clear example of the mind/body connection.

In addition, upbeat people tend to perform better. A positive attitude creates a feedback loop that becomes a self-fulfilling prophecy. People who think positively expect to perform well. They usually do and are rewarded with positive feedback. This reinforcement closes the loop. The positive results of *Mental Fitness Workouts* function the same way.

AGE SMART

MENTAL FITNESS WORKOUT
 # 4

RELAXATION WARM-UP
Follow the directions on Page 11.

MENTAL CALISTHENICS
C 4a Say your address and phone number, including zip and area codes aloud. Say your email address aloud. Repeat each backwards. Repeat whenever you have time with other people's data you know by heart. This is good training for your short-term memory.

C 4b Count up by 3 and down by 4 as quickly as you can. Start at 3 and 100.

$$3\text{-}100, 6\text{-}96, 9\text{-}92 \ldots 75\text{-}4$$

Repeat whenever you have time with numbers you choose.

SENSORY DRILLS
V 4 Look around you for $\sqrt{4}$, $\sqrt{\sqrt{7}}$, $\sqrt{\sqrt{\sqrt{10}}}$ triangular shaped objects. List the ones you find in your *MFJ*. You can do this exercise any time, anywhere. Look for objects to match criteria you select. Use different colors, sizes, functions: brown 4-legged animals, red cars, white scarves, furniture to sit on, etc.

As your powers of observation and concentration improve, make the exercise more challenging. Look for objects of uncommon colors and patterns or combinations of criteria, e.g., orange plaids, large red cubes.

To 4 Enter a familiar room with your eyes closed. Keep them closed and walk around the room. Identify aloud all the objects you touch. If you feel unsafe doing this by yourself, explain you are exercising to sharpen your sense of touch and ask someone to accompany you. Note the objects you correctly identify in your MFJ. Add the thoughts that came to mind as you did this exercise without being able to see.

ISOMETRICS

I 4 Estimate the number of lines in a paragraph in a book, a magazine, a newspaper, e.g., more than 12, less than 10, fewer than 6. How good an estimator are you? Repeat this exercise often until your estimates are pretty good.

VISUALIZATION

Vz 4 Visualize an area you can comfortably walk in 15-20 minutes. Draw a map of it according to a scale you devise. Include buildings, markers, signs, trees, cross-streets, etc.

SPRINTS

Sp 4 Name as many different head coverings as you can in 30 seconds.

MENTAL GYMNASTICS

MG 4 Copy the circles below exactly as they appear into your MFJ. Then, draw 4 straight lines through the circles without retracing or lifting your pencil from the paper.

    •   •   •

    •   •   •

    •   •   •

RESISTANCE TRAINING

RT 4 Read $\sqrt{1}$, $\sqrt{\sqrt{2}}$, $\sqrt{\sqrt{\sqrt{3}}}$ newspaper or magazine articles. In your MFJ, write a summary of the article/s.

MENTAL AEROBICS

MA 4 In two minutes, add a letter to each pair of letters below to form as many three-letter words as you can for each pair. Write the words you form in your MFJ.

HS	UR	ET
MN	BA	SD
IM	PT	OA

WEIGHT LIFTING

WL 4 Below are beginning and ending fragments of different stories. Write $\sqrt{1}$, $\sqrt{\sqrt{2}}$, $\sqrt{\sqrt{\sqrt{3}}}$ brief stories linking any beginning fragment to any ending fragment.

BEGINNINGS	ENDINGS
When I go to ...	... everyone woke up early.
At 6:00 PM when the ...	... there's no time to lose.
It's summer and ...	... when spring arrived.
It seems like the end of ...	... the crowd went wild.
It's getting colder and ...	... they were amazed.
The times have changed, the ...	... he appreciated that.
We have decided to...	... the police broke in.
Fortunately, ...	... it is hard to tell them.
Yesterday, as we were...	... and the children left.
Be very quiet ...	... then we ate some.
We are expecting a visit from...	... we went to see it.

STRETCHING

St 4 If you found a time capsule from 100 years ago, list 10-15 items you would like/expect to find. List 15-20 items you would put in a time capsule today.

CONSCIOUS RECALL

CR 4 Say the names of the first five presidents in order. Say the names of the last five presidents, starting with the most recent. Write the ten names in your MFJ.

COOL DOWN

In your MFJ, list 10 of your accomplishments. An accomplishment is anything you did well, enjoyed doing and are proud you did. It must meet all three criteria.

Accomplishments can be from any part of your life, any age, any activity. You will probably recall things you haven't thought about in years.

Now rank order the list, No. 1 being your major achievement. Write a full description of what you did to make each of your top three accomplishments happen.

From your descriptions, summarize your major strengths and satisfactions. Title this list "My Signal Strengths." You will refer to it in another *MFW*.

CONTROL THE WAY YOU AGE

The *Today* show is going to have many more Happy 100th Birthdays to celebrate. The Census Bureau created a new "100 plus" category because centenarians are the fastest growing population sector. Considering that the average life span at the turn of the 20th century was 46 years, we've come a long way - due primarily to improved medical treatment and sanitation.

AGING TODAY

The death of Mme. Jeanne Calment, August, 1997 in France at the age of 122, established the current life span, i.e., the maximum obtainable age. Eighty-five percent of people who live to be 100 years or more are women, 15 percent men.

Although fewer in number, men at this age are likely to be stronger physically and cognitively than the women in this cohort. The former didn't succumb to diseases and conditions that killed weaker men. Such data indicate women appear to be physiologically stronger and better able to cope with chronic illnesses and disabilities.

The next fastest growing age group comprises people between eighty-five and ninety-nine. By 2020, more kids will know and travel with their 80-something weight-lifting, course-taking great-grandparents as four-generation families become more common. We will also see more varied living arrangements; homo- or hetero-sexual couples together under one roof, under separate roofs or in late marriages.

At the turn of the 21st century, the NIA indicated people sixty-five and older were better able to live independently than they had been ten years earlier. Only 5.2 percent of the elderly were in nursing homes; 90 percent of those sixty-five to seventy-four had no disability; almost half of those eighty-five years of age were functional; and no more than 10 percent of those sixty-five to more than one hundred had Alzheimer's disease.

No one denies the cosmetic and physical changes that occur with aging – graying, thinner hair, wrinkled skin and thicker nails, arthritis, osteoporosis, poorer vision and/or hearing, heart and circulatory problems, diminished lung capacity, less efficient kidneys and bladder, a weaker immune system, even the loss of some mental processing speed. They're all part of the natural aging process.

However, mental changes often associated with aging - dementia, confusion, dullness - are *not* a natural part of the aging process. They are caused by disease, drugs, falls, bad habits, psychological trauma, or isolation and can be prevented, reversed or treated. The brain, if kept active, creates new connections among nerve cells where learning occurs and grows new message carriers - even as we age.

Aging is idiosyncratic. Everyone experiences it differently. Your friend may have no complaints; a neighbor, circulatory problems; a cousin, osteoporosis. Some centenarians have no disease until shortly before death. Within an individual, some systems may decline; others don't. You may have a hearing problem, but your blood pressure is fine. The onset and rate at which age-related change occurs varies among and within us.

YOU'RE IN CHARGE

According to John W. Rowe, M.D. and Robert L. Kahn, Ph.D., authors of *Successful Aging*, we control our own aging through the choices we make. How can that be? How can we control the inevitable?

The answer may surprise you. *Most of the unpleasant conditions attributed to advancing age are caused by life style choices you make - physically, mentally, emotionally, and behaviorally.* You begin to take charge of the way you age by attending to personal health and social matters.

1. *Be Sure You Are Physically Healthy*

Physical fitness is one of the three determinants of successful aging. Major contributing factors to physical fitness are diet, exercise and behavior, all of which you control. No one forces you to smoke, eat too much or eat the wrong foods. No one tells you not to exercise or become a couch potato. Those behaviors are all of your own choosing and, thus, within your power to change.

★ Have regular medical check ups. If you don't feel well or something is bothering you, don't ignore it; check it out. Ask to see another doctor if the physician you've been seeing isn't hearing what you are saying.

★ You are not being a hypochondriac if you go to the doctor when you do not feel right. You're being smart. It's your health, your aging, your life.

★ Have your vision and hearing tested, and make all prescribed corrections. How can you know what's going on - let alone remember it - when you don't see or hear clearly? Another important reason to have your vision checked at least once a year is to reduce your chances of falling (see below). If you're over sixty, have your eyes checked annually for glaucoma, an irreversible condition.

Although we access most data through vision and hearing, the remaining senses, smell, taste and touch, are important too. They add dimensions to experience, are important for personal safety and serve as excellent memory signposts.

★ Chronic olfactory impairment is a problem to some degree for half the adults over sixty-five. The sense of smell contributes significantly to the perception of flavor; therefore, deficits limit the enjoyment and too often, the intake of food. Doctors at John Hopkins note this could lead to malnutrition and depression. Other potential problems could be caused by insensitivity to spoiled food odors, personal body odors, smoke, and gas leaks.

★ Consult your health care provider about the loss of sensitivity in your fingers and toes. It could lead to serious burns or frost bite. Any diminished sensory acuity should be looked into. It could be a symptom of a serious medical condition

★ A medical exam can reveal thyroid, liver and kidney problems and conditions such as diabetes and dehydration, which can cause confusion, uncertainty and memory problems. Although such symptoms may seem mentally related, they could be caused by a physical ailment and corrected. That is why it is so important to have a complete medical check up.

The results of one study show the symptoms of 61 percent of patients with so-called "mental problems" disappeared once the cause, a physical disorder, was treated. If you or someone in your family is experiencing mental distress, insist upon a thorough physical examination as part of the diagnostic process.

★ High blood pressure, a common condition in older people, contributes to heart problems and strokes and reduces the oxygen supply to the brain. This can have a noticeably deleterious effect on mental acuity. Be sure to have your pressure monitored and kept under control through diet, exercise and/or drugs.

The bottom line is some mental states look very similar to dementia, but may be caused by physical problems. Dementia can't be cured, but many physical problems can be prevented and/or treated. All physical factors should be eliminated before a diagnosis of dementia is accepted.

2. *Exercise Regularly - No Matter Your Age*

NOTHING YOU CAN DO FOR YOURSELF IS MORE IMPORTANT TO YOUR TOTAL FITNESS THAN REGULAR PHYSICAL EXERCISE.

Evidence of its long-term, all-around value keeps mounting. In addition to the well-established significant cardiovascular and circulatory benefits, studies show exercise reduces the risk of falling; prevents bone loss; low-ers resting heart rate, blood pressure and "bad" cholesterol levels; eases the nausea and fatigue caused by cancer treatments; and increases a sense of well-being. Even older adults who suffer from painful knee os-teoarthritis, a prevalent ailment, enjoy better over-all health when they exercise.

The NIA reports exercise and physical activity can help prevent or delay some diseases and disabilities. They also can improve the health of people in their 90s, those who are frail and some who have diseases associated with aging. For some older adults, that may mean the ability to rise from a chair unaided and thus maintain their independ-ence longer.

Unfortunately, more than two thirds of this age group does not engage in regular physical activity. Don't be like them.

If an exercise program like the one in Chapter 6 below is not for you, consider a less structured approach. For example, 30 minutes per day of not strenuous movement prevents degeneration and increases muscle tone. Simply walking for that amount of time provides all the benefits noted above.

It is never too late to start. Even folks who begin in their 90s benefit. A study of men and women over seventy clearly shows a half hour of exercise, preferably daily, but at least three to five times a week, increases stamina, adds strength - making it easier to stand up and walk - builds bones, im-proves the immune system, and sharpens the mind.

Exercise benefits the brain primarily by improving blood flow. Not only does this increase the oxygen and nu-trients the brain needs to do its work, it increases levels of brain cell growth hormones. And, to reiterate, exercise is an excellent anti-depressant.

A 35-year study of men and women ages 55-80 indi-cated 30 minutes of aerobic and strength training exercises had the greatest effect on what were identified as "executive control functions," i.e., attention, organization and planning. A study from the University of Illinois-Urbana reveals physically fit men and women, 55-79, showed less age-related brain tissue shrinkage and a significant difference in cell communication in the regions of the brain affecting memory and learning.

3.   *Eat a Well-balanced, Low Fat, Low Cholesterol, High Fiber Diet*

As you age, you need fewer calories, but more nutrients. A well-balanced, low fat, low cholesterol diet is important for both physical health and mental fitness. Mental fitness profits from Vitamins B6, B12, and a B complex. They are needed to combat memory loss; to produce neurotransmitters, the chemicals that enable your brain cells to communicate so you can learn and remember; and to protect nerve fibers.

Your diet should feature six-to-eight 8-ounce glasses of water or other non-alcoholic beverages daily. Older people have a reduced sense of thirst; therefore, you may have to consciously remind yourself to drink enough fluid. An insufficient amount of water can negatively affect blood pressure, clotting and kidney functions.

The United States Department of Agriculture's new food pyramid includes a symbol of daily physical activity as a reminder of the dual importance and interrelatedness of physical exercise and diet to your overall health. Lack of exercise and poor diet are the second-largest underlying cause of death in the U.S.

USDA Dietary Guidelines

G   V   F O D M/B

Reading from left to right, the six food groups are Grains, Vegetables, Fruits, Oils, Dairy, and Meat/Beans. Your six or more servings per day of grains should come from fiber-full breads, cereals, rice, pasta, and dried beans. Your three or more daily servings of vegetables and fruit should be dark greens, reds, oranges, and yellows – the darker the better. Decrease your intake of saturated fats, and make your three calcium-rich dairy servings low fat. The two servings from the meat/beans group should be varied with an emphasis on fish, lean meat and poultry. "Make your plates plant centered," advises Kathie Swift, MS, RD.

The USDA suggests supplements of calcium and vitamin B-12 because it is difficult to obtain recommended amounts through diet, and supplements of vitamin D because of reduced, protected exposure to the sun. Also try to include foods rich in vitamins C and E and selenium because these antioxidants help to protect your immune system.

A few more tips. Just as you flavor your food, you should also savor it. Take your time while eating. Become aware of the textures and colors on your plate. Enjoy and appreciate your food. Dining is often a social activity. Relish it.

"Tell me what you eat and I will tell you what you are," said Anthelm Brillat-Savarin, French gourmet and lawyer, in 1825. It's not much different today.

4. *Stay Connected*

Okinawa, a Japanese archipelago in the Pacific Ocean, has the highest concentration of centenarians and the longest disability-free life span in the world. Okinawans don't smoke; eat a low fat, high fiber diet; drink alcohol in moderation; engage in daily physical activity; accentuate the positive; have stress-resistant personalities and high self-esteem; AND they enthusiastically participate in community group activities. This social engagement is a major feature of their culture and contributes significantly to their healthy longevity. Western research shows socially engaged men and women live longer, healthier lives than those without ties to family and friends.

People who are productively active, fully engaged and involved with others can see past themselves and evidence an inner sense of control. They see themselves as being in charge of what happens to them and their reactions. This characteristic enhances their self-esteem, which improves their mental fitness, both psychologically and physically.

Socializing with members of the opposite sex is a challenge for older people. Women far outnumber men sixty-five and older. Although the male-female ratio has been rising since 1990, the difference has not changed the social scene significantly. More older men than women are married; more older women live alone.

It is good to see older people, whether singly, in couples or groups, dining out, attending concerts, theatres and movies, volunteering, taking classes and workshops, pursuing their interests, enjoying themselves.

Social activity is better than staying home alone. Adopt statesman Bernie Baruch's motto, "Old age is always 15 years older than I am."

Social isolation is both numbing and dumbing. The fewer contacts you have, the less you do, the less active your mind, and the less you have to talk about. The less you have to say, the more difficult it becomes to converse, and the more awkward, less confident you feel. The less self-confidence you have, the more you shy away from contact with others. The less contact with others.... It is a vicious cycle. Don't get into it.

★ Get involved with whatever may interest you. If nothing comes to mind, or you're tired of what you've been doing, develop new interests. Despite what you may think, developing new interests is not that hard to do. You can find out about any subject at some level, regardless of how complicated an advance stage might be. You don't have to become an expert; "interested beginner" is a fine place to start.

★ Pursuing an interest engages your mind and is also a great way to meet people. Your common interest immediately gives you something to talk about, and if you are a newcomer to the field, you have the perfect opening gambit, "Would you please tell me about/how to...." People love to ride their hobbyhorses and talk about their interests - especially to someone who knows less than they.

Whether it's gardening, the internet, politics, or a cause you hold dear, use the subject to meet like-minded people. Join a club, association or organization. New members are always welcome. Volunteer to be on a committee; new workers are more than welcome. If you would like to volunteer on behalf of others and transcend yourself, hospitals, social services and schools always need help. Perhaps environmental or national organizations, such as the Peace Corps or Habitat for Humanity, appeal. Google "volunteer organizations" to discover many other organizations, even some abroad.

★ To find a new interest, try looking through magazines and journals in the library. Another good tactic is to read a book from the children's library on a subject of potential interest. It will give you an introductory, uncomplicated overview, and you can decide whether it interests you enough to continue. If you'd like to know more, books and articles will refer you to additional sources of information, including clubs and associations. You also can explore a world of interests online.

★ Test the waters with a friend or another newcomer to the field. That way you can share your enthusiasm, reinforce each other's interest and efforts and enjoy each other's support and encouragement. In addition, you won't have to worry about boring uninformed listeners. Plus you'll have someone to go to meetings with, since you'll both join the local chapter of a related organization.

★ Join a book group. New ones often are formed by your local book store or library.

★ Take a course in something you love or know nothing about. Learn to play bridge, arrange flowers, throw a pot, speak a foreign language, hybridize plants, play a musical instrument, square dance. The curriculum is endless.

★ Affiliate with an adult education or travel and learn program at a college or center near you. There are Learning In Retirement programs throughout the country. LIRs are a wonderful source of mental stimulation and social activity. Opportunities abound. Inquire, and take advantage of them.

No matter your age, it is possible to sharpen your mind, keep learning, improve your memory, think clearly, and make good decisions. At the same time, remaining active keeps you involved with people who are interested in what you like to do. It's a win-win situation. Successful aging is an on-going process. Keep it moving in the right direction.

5. *Get Help for Emotional Problems*

Depression is a serious problem that affects approximately 15 percent of older Americans. The incidence is understandable. Major causes of depression - serious illness, loss and disability - correlate with advancing age. Unfortunately, family and physicians too often attribute the symptoms of depression to stereotypic expectations of age and don't treat for it. On one survey, more than half the respondents 75 and older considered depression to be "normal."

An unfortunate corollary is the suicide rate among older adults, especially white males. It is significantly higher than for the rest of the population.

Depression may be the most prevalent mood disorder, but it is also the most treatable. The sadness caused by life events, great though it may be, is usually transient. After a period of grief and mourning, people tend to get on with their lives.

Chronic depression, however, is caused by biochemical changes. In addition to making you feel unhappy, inept and lethargic, chronic depression elevates levels of stress hormones and the accompanying harmful effects on your heart, blood pressure and brain. Chronic depression should be treated with medication. Professional talk-therapy plus a prescription seems to be a beneficial combination.

Stress is associated with illness and increased cognitive vulnerability. In addition to cardio-vascular problems, stress hormones slow the growth of new brain cells and increase the number of undesirable free radicals. People under stress manifest memory problems, lack of interest, confusion, and uncertainty. The symptoms make a false diagnosis of "possible dementia" quite possible. If you feel the effects of tension, anti-stress medications may be beneficial. Talk to your doctor about a trial prescription.

6. *Stop Smoking*

It is probably the most powerful behavioral health choice you can make with the greatest pay-off. Smoking is the number one underlying cause of death. As soon as you stop, you reduce the risk of heart attack; after ten years, you reduce the risk of lung cancer.

7. *Everything in Moderation*

Alcohol is the most abused drug in our society. Moreover, the older you are, the more susceptible you are to its inebriating effects. Four drinks now pack the same wallop as six drinks did when you were younger.

It may be tempting to try to lift your spirits or make the blues go away with a drink, but even if you perk up at first, alcohol is not a stimulant. It is a depressant. Be careful.

Reduce your intake - especially if you've been experiencing confusion or a lack of clarity. Alcohol contributes nothing positive to mental fitness.

However, red wine sales soared 15 years ago with reports it contained the antioxidants resveratrol and flavonoids, which protect the heart, may lessen the risk of diabetes and help people live longer. Studies about the alcohol-health connection have unclear results.

Harvard researchers believe no one alcoholic beverage is better for your health than any other and that how you imbibe is more important than what you drink. Since resveratrol is highly concentrated in grape skins, some scientists suggest it might be as heart healthy to drink dark grape juice, eat raisins and avoid alcohol's hazards.

So, what's a body to do? At this time, the consensus seems to be that a moderate amount of red wine consumed daily with food may help protect against certain cancers and heart disease and can have a positive effect on cholesterol levels and blood pressure. So, enjoy. If you take medications, though, be sure to explore possible interactions fully with your doctor.

8. *Get Enough Sleep*

Sleep is more fragmented with age. You may find yourself waking more often and for longer periods during the night, and your pattern may change. You may nap more frequently or find yourself going to bed earlier.

Sleep experts aren't sure if the need for sleep changes with age, but the ability to sleep changes for many people. Lack of sleep negatively affects mental fitness and memory. Not feeling well also affects the quality of sleep. If you are not sleeping well, see your health care provider about it.

9. *Have Your Meds Monitored*

Many medications make a mental mess. An inability to concentrate is not caused by aging *per se,* but poor concentration can be caused by a drug or combination of drugs. The 1979 Surgeon General's report noted many cases of apparent senility were actually caused by prescribed drugs, the interaction of prescribed drugs and/or the interaction of prescribed and over-the-counter (OTC) drugs.

Antihistamines, analgesics and anti-inflammatory, anti-nausea, and sleeping drugs cause drowsiness, fuzziness and fatigue. These medicinally induced states mimic mental deficiencies. An inability to concentrate, remember or think as well as you used to, may be the result of confusion caused by medications tested on healthy, younger subjects who tolerate, metabolize and eliminate meds differently. Medicinally induced confusion, dizziness and fatigue can also cause falls.

It is your responsibility to know which medications you take, why you take them, i.e., what they are supposed to do for you, and the correct dosage and frequency. Be sure to ask for a legible copy of any new prescription so you can verify it is filled correctly. The Institute of Medicine reports medication errors are surprisingly common; at least 1.5 million people a year are injured or killed in adverse drug events.

Doctors at New York's Mt. Sinai Hospital estimate average older adults regularly take four-to-five prescription meds, two OTC drugs and fill 12-17 prescriptions a year. In addition, many take herbal remedies for which no prescriptions are required. Medications and herbs can and do interact, not always favorably. According to one estimate, 80 percent of U.S. adults will use some combination of the above in any given week, and one-third will take five or more different medications.

To forestall adverse drug events, it is important that you create and maintain a legible, up-dated chart with the names, strength, dosage, and frequency of every prescribed and OTC medication, herbal remedy, vitamin and supplement you use. Take this chart with you whenever you go to the doctor or pharmacist.

It is also important to have one professional, your doctor or your pharmacist, know and monitor your entire drug regimen for content, correct dosage (potency levels vary with age and sex), possible interactions, unfavorable reactions, and adverse effects - including mental ones. It is also advisable to talk to your doctor about the possibility of reducing your meds.

Do your own research, too. For reputable information about drugs and supplements, use the National Institutes of Health web site, http://medlineplus.gov.

Like gerontologists who specialize in the care and treatment of older adults, there are "senior care" pharmacists. To find one near you, go to www.seniorcarepharmacist.com.

Buying drugs on the internet may offer financial savings, but it can be dangerous. Be sure you are dealing with legitimate online pharmacists. To locate Verified Internet Pharmacy Practice Sites, click on the Site Map at www.nabp.net, the National Association of Boards of Pharmacies web site. Be sure to tell your doctor or retail pharmacist about any drug purchased online. Everyone understands the desire to save money; there's no need to feel embarrassed by trying to economize.

10. *Avoid Falls*

Falls are now the number one cause of death from injury among seniors. Broken hips contribute markedly to loss of independence, medical problems and death.

Unfortunately, fear of falling causes many to avoid regular physical exercise. That is faulty thinking. *Physical exercise significantly helps reduce the risk of falling* because it improves balance and muscle strength.

As aging *per se* does not cause dementia, aging *per se* does not cause falls. They increase due to conditions related to age, but there is much you can do to attend to the risk factors involved.

Begin on a personal level. As stated above, carefully review your medications and have your vision checked annually.

In addition, <u>reduce</u> <u>hazards</u> in your home. Home is where we go to feel secure, but home is also where about half of all falls happen. After reading the suggestions below, do a hazards walk-through in your home and correct potential dangers.

★ Brighter lighting will help greatly. Be sure you can easily reach a light by your bed and keep a flashlight there, as well.

★ Arrange furniture so you have a clear walk-way. Tape wires and cords next to the walls so you don't trip over them. Remove clutter - books, boxes, shoes, clothing, anything you can trip over - from stairs and floors. Use double-sided tape to keep loose rugs from sliding.

★ Keep items you use often on lower cabinet and medicine chest shelves so you don't have to use step stools or ladders.

★ Be sure there are handrails on stairs and grab bars in the bathroom, as well as non-slip tub and shower mats.

★ Avoid going barefoot and wearing slippers or just socks. They slip and slide too easily.

★ Get up slowly from a chair or bed. It helps prevent dizziness and gives you time to focus.

★ Consider wearing an alarm device in case you do fall and need help.

We control the way we age through physical and pharmacological check-ups, by not smoking, by drinking alcohol moderately, eating well, exercising regularly, and maintaining an active social life. We may not be able to control every thing that happens to us, but we can control our choice of life style. Therefore, instead of passively letting the years pass, age pro-actively: *Age Smart.*

AGE SMART

MENTAL FITNESS WORKOUT
5

RELAXATION WARM-UP
Follow the directions on Page 11.

MENTAL CALISTHENICS
C 5a Spell the complete names – first, middle, last – of everyone in your family aloud. Then do it backwards.

C 5b As quickly as possible, count up by 2, down by 2, starting at 2 and 100:

2-100, 4-98, 6-96, 8-94 ... 100- 2

Count up by 3, down by 3, starting at 3 and 100:

3- 100, 6-97, 9-94, 12-91 ... 99-1

Great mini-mental massage. Repeat often using numbers you choose.

SENSORY DRILLS
A 5 Listen to a 15-minute news program. In your MFJ,
   √   Record every number you hear during the broadcast. Include dates, times, station frequencies, money....
   √√ Record every number, color and person's name you hear.
   √√√ Record numbers, colors, personal names and locations.
√,√√,√√√, Summarize the lead story.

Ta 5 Eat something in each of the four basic taste groups: sweet, salty, sour, and bitter. Describe the taste sensations in your MFJ.

ISOMETRICS

I 5 Draw mirror images of the following figures.

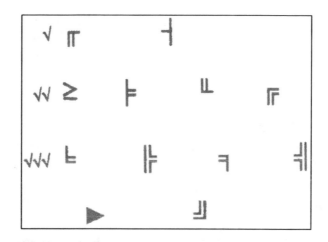

VISUALIZATION

Vz 5 Begin to estimate the size of objects - pens, glasses, books, plates, rooms, distances – to enhance your visual-spatial awareness. Monitor your accuracy in your MFJ.

SPRINTS

Sp 5 Say as many words beginning with the letter "g" as you can in 30 seconds. Repeat this mini-mental massage often, using any letter you choose.

MENTAL GYMNASTICS

MG 5 All but one of the three-digit numbers in the box below has a feature in common. Look at them for 20 seconds, then try to find the "uncommon" number in less than √45, √√30, √√√15 seconds. Write the number and time it took you to find it in your MFJ.

594

276

495

363

374   165

891

792

682

583

396

RESISTANCE TRAINING

RT 5 Look out the window for √5, √√10, √√√15 minutes. Record everything you see in your MFJ.

MENTAL AEROBICS

MA 5 In your MFJ, write as many associations as you can for each of the following stimulus words. Example: SUN: hot, summer, beach, swim, ocean, boat, fish........

√	√√	√√√
TREE	DESK	DINNER
MOVIES	HORSE	SHOES
SNOW	PENCIL	LAMP
	UMBRELLA	HOTEL
		WINDOW
		CAULIFLOWER
		COMPUTER

WEIGHT LIFTING

WL 5 Unscramble the following words and write them correctly in your MFJ.

√ inale, rgnya, sbtal, iplso, rmien, fcatr

√√ gesnil, mlonra, vehrit, vtocra, negalt, rmerot, osensa, ytisfas

√√√ briteelr, uloccend, cpilatarc, debailmar, ohmaioruns, haeprmsote, spibeoisml, cnitilioann, vtaeiynetlt, nhighlwtoid

STRETCHING

St 5 Make up definitions for these nonsense words: corflung, slajinc, pryglid, urstile

CONSCIOUS RECALL

CR 5 Name five mountain ranges in the world. What is the highest mountain on earth?

COOL DOWN

For the Chapter 3 *Cool Down,* you identified characteristics of Mental Fitness "Needing Improvement" and noted them in your MFJ. How are you doing? Assess your progress.

Recall incidents when you believe you demonstrated improvement and/or those when you think you still might do better. Describe them in your MFJ. Focus your attention on improving these aspects of your Mental Fitness Profile.

We do not stop playing because we age;
we age because we stop playing.
Anonymous

PHYSICAL FITNESS - SAFE, SMART

If you are of a certain age, chances are you grew up pre-spas, co-ed gyms, sexy exercise instructors on TV, CDs, DVDs, sports bras, and latex shorts. It's not that you don't know physical exercise is good for you, but back then only jocks did it. Older adults certainly didn't think the idea applied to them. Today, we know it definitely does and for several reasons.

IT'S FUN AND FEELS GOOD

1. Exercise makes you more alert.
2. Exercise gets you in better shape to do and profit from mental exercise.
3. Mental fitness depends on the increased flow of blood, oxygen and nutrients to the brain generated by physical activity.
4. Exercising with others is a productive social activity.
5. Exercise is fun and makes you feel good.
6. Physical exercise is the quickest, most direct drug-free way into a better mood.
7. Not too many practices can make all these claims.

Although movement, exercise and activity are among the strongest tools people have at their disposal to help them stay healthy, some are afraid they will be too strenuous or harmful and are reluctant to try. But studies show some exercise is safe for people of all ages, and older adults hurt themselves far more by *not* exercising than by exercising.

Think about making a one-month commitment to exercise. If you increase your physical activity for 30 days, it's a pretty good sign you'll probably keep it up. "Maybe," you say, "but what's going to keep me from quitting as I have in the past?"

First, frame your mental message positively. Tell yourself it's a fun way to be good to yourself. Program your brain to keep reminding you that exercise is the master key to physical and mental fitness.

Secondly, you're more likely to keep at it now you're reassured exercise is safe at your age; once you learn what exercises to do and how to do them correctly; once they become a regular part of your routine; and you see improvement within a fairly short time.

Thirdly, there's a lot to choose from. You can join a club or gym, work out with a friend, hire a trainer, or follow the NIA's physical fitness program designed for adults (see below) at home, at your convenience.

Regardless of your choice, dress in comfortable layers and wear good, padded athletic shoes with arch supports. Sturdy footwear is particularly important for older exercisers with arthritis. If you need new shoes, be sure to measure your feet before buying; your foot size can change with age. Shop for shoes at the end of the day when your feet are at their largest, and don't settle for ones that hurt. It's unlikely the discomfort will ease up with wear. Break the shoes in easily to avoid blisters, especially if you have diabetes.

As people get older, they often don't have the urge to drink – even though they need to. Drink fluids – water, athletic beverages – when you do any activity, especially one that makes you sweat. To keep the engine fueled, eat nutrient heavy, calorie light food - the less fats, oils and sweets, the better.

First, Consult Your Doctor if You Have

> Any new, undiag-
>   nosed symptom/s
> Chest pain
> Irregular, rapid or
>   fluttery heart beat
> Severe shortness of
>   breath
> Ongoing, significant,
>   undiagnosed weight
>   loss
> Joint swelling

> Persistent pain or
>   problems walking af-
>   ter a fall; there might
>   be a break you don't
>   know about
> A hernia causing pain
>   and discomfort
> Foot or ankle sores
>   that won't heal
> Eye conditions
> An acute blood clot

THE NATIONAL INSTITUTE ON AGING
PHYSICAL FITNESS PROGRAM

If movements in this workout are unfamiliar and seem strange at first, don't worry, you'll get used to them. Make sure your shoulders and hips are square while you're exercising, i.e., you're not twisting your body; your legs are somewhat bent if you're standing; and your back is in a neutral position. Look at yourself in the mirror to check that your body is in alignment.

Although the illustrations below show men doing some exercises and women doing other ones, all the exercises can be done by both sexes.

An inactive lifestyle can penalize you in four areas important for health and independence: Strength, Balance, Flexibility, and Endurance. Doing exercises that target these areas will help maintain or even partly rejuvenate them.

STRENGTH EXERCISES counteract weakened muscles, which enables you to do more on your own; increase your metabolism, which helps keep your weight and blood sugar under control; and may help prevent osteoporosis.

❖ Don't hold your breath during strength exercises. This could affect your blood pressure.

❖ Breathe out as you lift or push a weight; breathe in as you relax.

❖ Use smooth, steady movements.

❖ Avoid jerking or thrusting movements.

❖ Avoid locking the joints of your arms and legs into a strained position.

❖ Muscle soreness lasting a few days and slight fatigue are normal after muscle building exercises.

❖ Exhaustion, sore joints, and painful muscle pulls are not normal results of exercising.

1) Arm Raises strengthen your shoulder muscles.
1. Sit in a chair with your back straight.
2. Keep feet flat on the floor even with your shoulders.
3. Hold hand weights straight down at your sides with palms facing inward.

- You can use as little as 1- or 2-pound hand weights or you can substitute cans of soup. Some people start without weights.
- Take three (3) seconds to lift or push a weight into place. Hold the position for one (1) second, and take another three (3) to lower it. Don't let the weight drop – lowering it slowly is very important.

4. Raise both arms to the side, shoulder height.
5. Hold the position for 1 second.

6. Slowly lower arms to the sides. Pause.
7. Repeat 8 to 15 times.
8. Rest. Do another set of 8-15 repetitions.

2) Chair Stands strengthen stomach and thigh muscles.
1. Place pillows against back of chair.
2. Sit in middle or toward front of chair, knees bent, feet flat on floor.
3. Lean back on pillows in half-reclining position, keeping your back and shoulders straight.

4. Raise upper body forward until sitting upright, using hands as little as possible — or not at all, if you can. Your back should no longer lean against the pillows.
5. Slowly stand up, using hands as little as possible.
6. Slowly sit back down. Keep back and shoulders straight throughout exercise.
7. Repeat 8 to 15 times. Rest. Then repeat 8 to 15 times more.

3) Bicep Curls strengthen upper-arm muscles.
1. Sit in armless chair. Keep feet flat and even with shoulders.
2. Hold hand weights at sides, arms straight, palms facing toward your body.
3. Slowly bend one elbow, lifting weight toward chest. Be sure to rotate palm to face shoulder while lifting weight.
4. Hold position for 1 second. Slowly lower arm to starting position.
5. Repeat with other arm. Alternate until you have repeated the exercise 8 to 15 times on each side.
6. Rest. Then do another set of 8 to 15 alternating repetitions.

4) Tricep Extensions strengthen muscles in the back of the arm.

1. Sit near the front edge of the chair, feet flat on floor and even with shoulders.
2. Hold a weight in one hand, raise that arm straight toward the ceiling, palm facing in.
3. Support arm below the elbow with the other hand.

4. Slowly bend raised arm at elbow, bringing hand weight toward same shoulder.
5. Slowly re-straighten arm toward ceiling.
   Hold position for 1 second.
6. Slowly bend arm toward shoulder again.
7. Pause, then repeat the bending and straightening until you have done the exercise 8 to 15 times. Repeat 8 to 15 times with your other arm.
8. Rest. Then repeat another set of 8 to 15 repetitions on each side.

5) Knee Flexion strengthens muscles in the back of the thigh.

1. Stand straight, holding onto table or chair for balance.
2. Slowly bend one knee as far as possible, so foot lifts up behind you. Don't move your upper leg at all; bend your knee only.
3. Hold position.
4. Slowly lower foot all the way back down.
5. Repeat with other leg.
6. Alternate legs until you have 8 to 15 repetitions with each leg. Rest.
7. Then do another set of 8 to 15 alternating repetitions.

HOW MUCH, HOW OFTEN?

Do strength exercises for all your major muscle groups at least twice a week. Don't do strength exercises of the same muscle group on any two (2) days in a row.

Depending on how fit you are, you might need to start out using as little as 1-2 pounds of weight, or no weight at all, to allow your body to adapt to strength exercises. Soup cans or filled plastic bottles make good weights. It should feel somewhere between hard and very hard for you to lift or push the weight. It should not feel *too* hard.

Lift a minimum of weight at the beginning. If you can't lift or push a weight eight (8) times in a row, it's too heavy for you; reduce the amount of weight. If you can lift a weight comfortably more than 15 times in a row, it's too light for you; increase it. You need a challenging amount of weight to benefit from strength exercises. If you don't gradually challenge your muscles, you won't get stronger.

While you are resting between sets, you might want to stretch the muscle you just worked or do a different strength exercise that uses a different set of muscles.

BALANCE EXERCISES build leg muscles and help prevent falls. Each year, U.S. hospitals have 300,000 admissions for broken hips, and falling is often the cause of those fractures. Balance exercises can help you stay independent by helping you avoid disabilities that may result from falling.

There is a lot of overlap between strength and balance exercises. Lower body exercises for strength also help balance.

SAFETY TIPS

❖ Hold onto a table or chair for balance with only one hand. As you progress, try holding on with only one fingertip.

❖ Next, try the following exercises without holding on at all. You may want to ask someone to watch you the first few times in case you lose your balance.

❖ If you are very steady on your feet, move on to doing the exercises using no hands, with your eyes closed. Have someone stand close by if you are unsteady.

❖ Breathe out as you lift your legs. Breathe in as you lower them.

1) Side Leg Raises strengthen muscles at sides of hips and thighs.

1. Stand straight, directly behind table or chair, feet slightly apart.
2. Hold table or chair for balance.
3. Slowly lift one leg to side, 6 to 12 inches out to the side. Keep your back and both legs straight. Don't point your toes downward – keep them facing forward. Hold position.
4. Slowly lower leg. Repeat with other leg.
5. Keep back and knees straight throughout exercise.
6. Alternate legs until you repeat exercise 8 to 15 times with each leg.
7. Rest. Do another set of 8 to 15 alternating repetitions.

2) Hip Flexion strengthens thigh and hip muscles.

Use ankle weights when you are ready.

1. Stand straight; hold onto a table or chair for balance.
2. Slowly bend one knee toward chest, without bending waist or hips.
3. Hold position for 1 second.
4. Slowly lower leg all the way down. Pause.
5. Repeat with other leg.
6. Alternate legs until you have done 8 to 15 repetitions with each leg.
7. Rest; then do another set of 8 to 15 alternating reps.
8. Add modifications as you progress.

3) Hip Extension strengthens buttock and lower-back muscles.

Use suitable ankle weights when you are ready.
Don't start out with weights that are too heavy.

1. Stand 12 to 18 inches from a table or chair, feet slightly apart.

2. Bend forward at hips at about 45-degree angle; hold onto a table or chair for balance.
3. Slowly lift one leg straight backwards without bending your knee, pointing your toes, or bending your upper body any farther forward.
4. Hold position for 1 second.
5. Slowly lower leg. Pause.
6. Repeat with other leg.
7. Alternate legs until you have done 8 to 15 repetitions with each leg.
8. Rest; then do another set of 8 to 15 alternating repetitions.
9. Add modifications as you progress.

4) Anytime-Anywhere exercises improve your balance.

You can do them almost anytime, anywhere, and as often as you like, as long as you have something sturdy nearby to hold onto if you become unsteady.

❖ Walk heel-to-toe. Position your heel just in front of the toes of the opposite foot each time you take a step. Your heel and toes should touch or almost touch.

❖ Stand on one foot (for example, while waiting in line at the grocery store or at the bus stop). Alternate feet.

❖ Stand up and sit down without using your hands.

Check your progress:

1. Time yourself as you stand on one foot, without support, for as long as possible.
2. Stand near something sturdy to hold onto in case you lose your balance.
3. Repeat the test while standing on the other foot.
4. Test and record your scores each month on the grid below.

HOW MUCH, HOW OFTEN?

Don't do more than your regularly scheduled strength exercise sessions to incorporate these balance modifications; it can do more harm than good to do strength exercises too often. Simply do your strength exercises and incorporate these balance techniques as you progress.

STRETCHING EXERCISES are planned to give you more freedom of movement to do the things you need and like to do. Stretching exercises alone will not improve your endurance or strength. They may, however, help keep your body limber, prevent injuries and falls or hasten recovery from injuries.

SAFETY TIPS

- ❖ Always warm up before stretching exercises. That means do them <u>after</u> endurance or strength exercises or by doing some easy walking or arm-pumping first.
- ❖ Stretching should never cause pain, especially joint pain.
- ❖ Mild discomfort or a mild pulling sensation is normal.
- ❖ Never bounce into a stretch — make slow steady movements instead.
- ❖ Stretch into the desired position as far as possible without pain.

1) Tricep Stretches lengthen muscles in the back of the upper arm.

1. Hold one end of a towel in right hand.

2. Raise and bend right arm to drape towel down back. Keep your right arm in this position and continue holding onto the towel.

3. Reach behind your lower back and grasp bottom end of towel with left hand.

4. Climb left hand progressively higher up towel, which also pulls your right arm down. Continue until your hands touch, or get as close as you can comfortably go.

5. Reverse positions.

6. Repeat 3 to 5 times each session. Hold stretch for 10 to 30 seconds. Relax, then repeat, trying to stretch farther.

2) Double Hip Rotation stretches the outer muscles of hips and thighs.

Don't do this exercise if you have had a hip replacement, unless your surgeon approves.

1. Lie on floor on your back, knees bent and feet flat on the floor.

2. Keep shoulders on floor at all times.

3. Keep knees bent together and gently lower legs to one side as far as possible without forcing them.

4. Hold position for 10 to 30 seconds.

5. Return legs to upright position.

6. Repeat toward other side.

7. Repeat 3 to 5 times on each side. Each time, try to stretch farther.

HOW MUCH, HOW OFTEN?

Stretch after you do your regularly scheduled strength and endurance exercises. If you can't do endurance or strength exercises for some reason, and stretching exercises are the only kind you are able to do, do them at least 3 times a week, for at least 20 minutes each session. Reminder: stretching exercises, by themselves, don't improve endurance or strength.

ENDURANCE EXERCISES are activities — walking, jogging, swimming, raking — that increase your heart rate and breathing for an extended period of time. Endurance exercises improve the health of your heart, lungs and circulatory system. They also may delay or prevent diseases such as diabetes, colon cancer, heart disease, osteoporosis, and stroke. Not only do endurance exercises improve your health, they can also improve your stamina for tasks you need to do to live independently.

Build up your endurance gradually, starting with as little as 5 minutes of endurance activities at a time, if you need to. Examples of moderate endurance activities for the average older adult are listed below. Older adults who have been inactive for a long time will need to work up to these activities gradually.

❖ Walking briskly on a level surface
❖ Swimming
❖ Gardening, mowing, raking
❖ Cycling on a stationary bicycle
❖ Bicycling.

The following are examples of activities that are vigorous. These activities are not for people who have been inactive for a long time or who have certain health risks.

❖ Climbing stairs or hills
❖ Brisk bicycling up hills
❖ Digging holes.

Gradually working your way up is especially important if you have been inactive for a long time. It may take months to go from a very long-standing sedentary lifestyle to doing some of the activities suggested in this section.

SAFETY TIPS

- ❖ Stretch after your activities, when your muscles are warm.
- ❖ Drink water.
- ❖ Dress appropriately for the heat and cold.
- ❖ To prevent injuries, use safety equipment such as helmets for biking.
- ❖ Endurance activities should not make you breathe so hard that you can't talk and should not cause dizziness or chest pain.

HOW MUCH, HOW OFTEN?

Your goal is to work your way up to a moderate-to-vigorous level that increases your breathing and heart rate. It should feel somewhat difficult to you. Once you reach your goal, you can divide your exercise into sessions of no less than 10 minutes at a time, if you want to, as long as they add up to a total of at least 30 minutes on most or all days of the week.

Doing less than 10 minutes at a time won't give you the desired cardiovascular and respiratory system benefits. The exception to this guideline is when you first make the decision to begin endurance activities, and you are just starting out.

TRACK YOUR PROGRESS

Copy the grid below in your MFJ. Use it to track your progress in endurance, lower-body power, strength, and balance. Seeing evidence of your progress will motivate continued effort on your part. To get a baseline score, test yourself before you begin this program. Then test and record your scores every two weeks.

For endurance exercises, see how far you can walk in exactly six minutes. Write down the distance – in blocks, laps, miles, number of times you walked up and down a long hallway, or whatever is convenient for you.

For lower-body strength, time yourself as you walk up a flight of stairs as fast as you can safely. For upper-body strength exercises, record how much weight you lift and how many times you lift that weight.

For balance exercises, time yourself as you stand on one foot, without support, for as long as possible. Stand near something sturdy to hold onto in case you lose your balance. Repeat the test while standing on the other foot.

PHYSICAL FITNESS PROGRESS RECORD

	Base	J	F	M	A	M	J	J	A	S	O	N	D
Endurance Distance													
Power Time													
Strength Wt./Reps													
Balance Time Right Left													

AGE SMART
MENTAL FITNESS WORKOUT
6

RELAXATION WARM-UP
Follow the directions on Page 11.

MENTAL CALISTHENICS
C 6a Spell the days of the week aloud. Spell them backwards aloud. Say them in alphabetical order.

C 6b Count aloud from 1-100 while writing the numbers in descending order from 100-1.

SENSORY DRILLS
V 6 Go on a Scavenger Hunt at home. List the items you find in your MFJ.

√	√√	√√√	
Blue Box	Blue Box	Blue Box	Gold Jewelry
Red Ball	Red Ball	Red Ball	Green Dish
Aqua Cup	Aqua Cup	Aqua Cup	Purple Button
Yellow Fruit	Yellow Fruit	Yellow Fruit	Brown Bag
White Pencil	White Pencil	White Pencil	Silver Pen
Pink Ribbon	Pink Ribbon	Pink Ribbon	Beige Thread
	Black Case	Black Case	Orange Book
	Beige Thread		
	Orange Book		

To 6 Do your complete teeth brushing routine with your eyes closed. What required the most attention? Record your answers in your MFJ.

ISOMETRICS
I 6

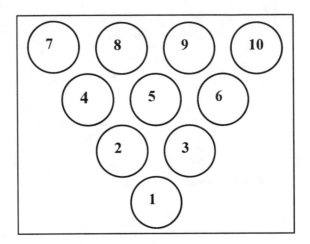

Study the figure. By moving only three circles, you can turn the pyramid upside down. Which three are they? Write their numbers in your MFJ.

VISUALIZATION

Vz 6 Visualize and draw a floor plan of the first house or apartment you lived in after you left school or your parents' home. Add furniture, lamps, fixtures, decorations, floor coverings, window treatments, wall hangings. Use colored pencils/crayons. Try to draw to a scale you devise.

SPRINTS

Sp 6 In one minute, name $\sqrt{10}$, $\sqrt{\sqrt{15}}$, $\sqrt{\sqrt{\sqrt{25}}}$ useful tools to have around the house.

MENTAL GYMNASTICS

MG 6 Unscramble the following word triangles, and write the correctly spelled words in your MFJ

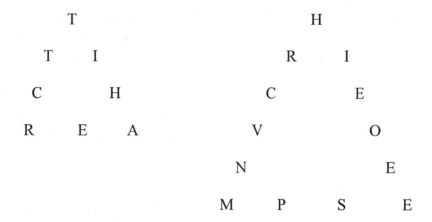

RESISTANCE TRAINING

RT 6 In your MFJ, write the opposites of the following words backwards. For example, OFF – NO

WHITE	DARK	CEILING	DAY	BAD
SHORT	SAD	BIG	UGLY	ODD

MENTAL AEROBICS

MA 6 Copy the words below into your MFJ. Group them into categories. Label the categories and arrange them in a logical hierarchy.

Flower, Wren, Animal, Pear, Living Matter, Dog, Fruit, Terrier, Vegetable, Canary, Apple, Rose, Bird, Daisy, Collie

WEIGHT LIFTING

WL 6 Look at the words below for $\sqrt{60}$, $\sqrt{\sqrt{45}}$, $\sqrt{\sqrt{\sqrt{30}}}$ seconds. Write as many as you can remember in your MFJ.

Look at the words again for as long as you did last time. Now, quickly form associations with as many as you can, and write them your MFJ.

Repeat writing the words and associations as many times as it takes to get them all right.

Write a brief story incorporating as many of the words below as you can. Write a story using the associations you formed. Compare the stories.

OCEAN   **ROTATE**   foreign   BOULEVARD

station   *conference*   attractive   GLASS   PARROT

SIMPLE   **moon**   *RESTAURANT*   *PIZZA*

ALPHABET   SAXOPHONE   *COMPUTER*

STRETCHING

St 6 Role play "Travel Agent." Plan the itinerary of a trip you, as a client, would like to make. Choose the destination, the best time to go, how you would get there, where you would stay. Describe the clothing you would need to bring, stages of the trip, sites you would visit, how long you'd stay at each site; attractions you would be sure to see and why; anticipated activities at each of the stops; if money were no object, purchases you would like to make. Bon Voyage......

CONSCIOUS RECALL

CR 6 Draw your immediate family tree. Start with your grandparents and take it down to your grandchildren or great-grandchildren.

COOL DOWN

Review the Signal Strengths you identified in the Chapter 4 *Cool Down*. Think about how you might apply them in helping you affect the way you age. In your MFJ, describe how you can build on your strengths to age well.

MEMORY MINDERS

Where are my keys? My glasses? The car? What's that word, that name? It's on the tip of my tongue....

Sound familiar? Probably. It happens to all of us. Every one forgets – at *every* age. When children forget their gloves, we say, "Of course. They're only children. What do you expect?" When adolescents forget to call, we say, "Of course. They're teenagers. What do you expect?" When 20-, 30-, 40-year olds forget an appointment, we say, "Of course. They're so busy - college, job, house, family. What do you expect?"

Why is it then, when we forget, which does happen more often after ages 45-50, we get nervous? We start to worry about "losing it." When 50-year olds forget something, they say, "I must be getting old." And 60-year olds who forget something silently wonder if it's the first sign of Alzheimer's disease. We remember much more than we think.

You forget how much you remember. To see how much you really know about memory, try *Your Aging I.Q.* adapted from the NIA.

YOUR AGING I.Q.

Enter T or F in your MFJ.

1. Medications can affect memory.
2. People of all ages forget.
3. Writing things down is a cop out that weakens memory.
4. Getting older leads to senility.
5. Forgetting can be caused by not paying attention.
6. Short term memory refers to things that happened yesterday.
7. Recall slows as people age.
8. Vision or hearing problems can affect memory.
9. Mental exercise can prevent memory loss.
10. Older people can do as well as younger people on cognitive ability tests.

The correct answers are at the end of *MFW* 7.

THE 3 Rs

Memory is not an isolated, independent operation. How much you remember is affected by the significance and emotional overlay of the content, how tired you are and any inhibitions you may have. Memory is also closely related to the amount of attention you pay, your perceptions, the level of your intelligence, and the strength of your imagination.

Part of the brain's genius lies in not making memory a one-step, all-or-nothing function. In addition to the 3Rs you studied in school, are Memory's 3Rs: Register, Record and Retrieve. Each phase has its methodology. As a result, memory cooperatively provides junctures where you can intervene and improve it by targeting your exercises.

To facilitate the intricacies of the process, memory uses and depends upon the mental muscles you have been exercising. Strong muscles of the mind strengthen memory. An improved memory enhances mental fitness.

REGISTER/ACQUIRE DATA: To say you are aware of something, you must perceive a stimulus and apprehend data. Data not perceived, cannot be acquired, let alone remembered. The exercises you have been doing to sharpen your sensory acuity and perception and improve your ability to focus your attention reinforce this important stage of memory. You can make significant improvements at this level.

Memory is nourished by our senses. All external input to the brain comes from them, and sense impressions function as good clues for retrieval. The more senses involved, the stronger the imprint and the easier you remember. When you really want to remember something, work your senses and commit the scene to memory. Purposefully observe the setting, images, colors, sounds, aromas; if applicable, use taste and touch too. The more sensory input, the better your chances of recall.

Sensation precedes reasoning and may be entwined with emotion, the physical response to sense generated data. The deeper the emotion, the more powerful the memory. Undoubtedly, you recall exactly where you were on 9/11. Unfortunately, senses are often diminished by habit and poor maintenance; therefore, it is your responsibility to sharpen yours, reawaken any dulled ones, and habitually use sensory landmarks to facilitate retention and cue recall.

Probably nothing improves memory more than PAYING ATTENTION. Staying focused overcomes obstacles that obstruct registering. PAYING ATTENTION requires discipline and active involvement. When you are alert and aware, you have a better grasp of what is happening, and you feel more self-confident. Positive reinforcement is its own reward.

Initially, whatever touches your awareness is translated into temporary pathways of nerve cell activity called short-term memory. STM has about a 30-second span, a

7-digit capacity. Pre-area code phone numbers were seven figures; you were able to keep the number in mind or keep repeating it, until you made the call or wrote it down.

STMs are supposed to be fleeting because new ones are constantly replacing them. That is beneficial - you can discard what you don't really need and focus on what is important.

As such, STMs are fragile and easily dislodged by interruptions. That is why it is so easy to forget what you're doing or thinking when something intervenes; why you can't remember why you came into the room or why you have to go back and start counting all over - from the beginning - when you've been distracted.

One way to improve STM is to chunk data. Your area code may contain three digits - 617, 541, 785 - but to your brain, it really is only one bit of information. Research indicates workable chunks are about seven digits, six letters and five words.

The term "Working Memory" is sometimes interchanged with STM; however, the latter is much shorter. Although both have limited capacity, WM usually denotes the temporary storage and manipulation of information. A better title might be "working attention."

RECORD/RETAIN: Retention or long-term memory (LTM) is the mechanism by which material is consolidated and archived on strengthened neural pathways. Language is integral to retention. It resists the passage of time and enables us to reinforce what we want to remember.

LTM is who you are, the sum total of all you remember, as well as your capacity for remembering. No one's LTM has ever been known to max out. There's always room to learn and store more.

LTM takes up more of the brain and is less fragile than STM. You still have childhood memories of grandma's freshly baked cookies and flashbacks to your first romance. Such memories last because they involve many parts of the brain and are laden with affect.

In LTM, the brain consolidates and structures incoming data. Your left brain organizes information methodically, rationally - by category, by hierarchy. It associates the new with data already in place. This reinforces your ability to adapt to new situations in daily living, to get a handle on what's happening. Without LTM, everything would seem to be happening the first time; you would constantly have to re-learn. We attribute this rational approach to our culture and formal education.

Logic, however, is not the only way to order memory. Your right brain forms intuitive, holistic associations that are fluid, imaginative and idiosyncratic. No one has had the same mix of experiences as you or makes the same associations. Linkages may be based on personal events, sensations, memories, relationships, ideas, or connections only your mind would make.

Imagination is involuntary and trumps rational processes. Mental images are retained better than words or sounds and are more easily recalled. One picture is worth thousands of words.

Strong long-term memories are those that were completely encoded, i.e., you were paying attention, and/or they had emotional impact. We are more likely to retain new information when we can relate it to older, more-established memories. Consciously creating personal associations, connecting the new you want to remember to old personally meaningful links, is an effective way to improve your memory.

Some scientists believe a good night's sleep seals memories. They believe dreaming strengthens the nerve paths that encode LTMs. Students may do the infamous all-nighter, but they will do better to study for a test and go to sleep immediately to help retain the material.

There are different kinds of LTMs. Explicit memories are the result of conscious efforts to learn material and recall it at will - telephone numbers, historical dates, scientific facts and figures, much of what you were tested on at school. This is the most troublesome type of memory to recall for people as they age.

Implicit memory is procedural. We use it automatically - to dress, ride bikes, drive a car. Certain foods and odors trigger implicit memories of family dinners, holidays, vacations; often they have strong emotional overtones.

Semantic memories are facts we had to deliberately learn but have become so deeply ingrained they surface without effort - the alphabet, family names, multiplication tables, the pledge of allegiance.

RETRIEVE/RECALL: Nerve pathways take less than a second to reactivate LTMs. "Is this coat yours?" It takes 1/5 of a second for the image to reach your brain, 1/5 for you to decide, 1/5 to reply. More complicated matters take longer, of course, but timing varies directly with familiarity. The brain tries to reactivate the neuronal pathways that encoded information related to what you are trying to remember. If the pathways are intact, the memory is retrievable and will surface - at some point.

Active recall is the main issue for people over 50. It's that Tip-of-the-Tongue phenomenon. We remember, we just can't spit it out.

Memory is the electrical and chemical storage and retrieval of experiences. Where is it located? In no one place. Events are not stored as wholes. Rather, the material is broken into its components, which are stored in specialized areas distributed across the brain. Different areas process sights, sounds, smells, arrangements, sequencing, height. When you remember a song, for example, the words and melody are stored in different parts of your brain.

When you want to recall something, it's necessary to assemble the various bits and pieces that make up the memory, coordinate and combine them. It involves busy, dynamic multi-tasking. That is why memories never play back as exact replications of the event; why two "eye-witness" reports can vary; and why each time the event is recalled, it's not exactly the same as a previous recollection.

Memories continually change over time. They're re-shaped and re-remembered. Actually, when you remember something - unless it's the first time - you are probably remembering your previous memory of the event.

Retrieval is a complex process. It is difficult to mentally search for data, locate and extract it. That is why you should take advantage of retrieval cues. As noted above, memory works through associations - logical or intuitive, conscious or unconscious, intended or passive. Train yourself to use clues to forge links.

Spatial clues relate to physical orientation. Consciously note locations, activities, colors, sounds, aromas, textures to guide recall. When looking for objects, retrace your steps. When trying to remember written matter, recreate the last time you saw it; visualize the sheet of paper, where you were, what was playing on the radio, what you were wearing. Some people subconsciously recall the placement of a name on a page. It's useful to deliberately try to do that.

Temporal cues aren't tangible. Because they can only be represented, it is more difficult to position yourself in time. However, sequencing events helps to remember and recall them. Adopt a mental perspective of the past and future. Visualize how events transpired to enhance the memory.

Conscious linkage is the deliberate attempt to extract a desired memory. It involves reaching deep for whatever associations you can come up with to act as guides, sign-posts, landmarks, and clues. Your ability to work your mental muscles strengthens your memory and gives you access to the data you seek.

Unfortunately, forgetting occurs as soon as data are re-tained - at any age. Developing clue-making skills will improve your ability to locate, recruit and retrieve the data you want.

As you can see, "memory" is one word for a compli-cated, multi-stage process. To improve your memory, you need to address each phase. You have to stimulate, develop and reinforce the underlying mechanisms. You must learn to use associations, clues and devices. If you memorize a poem, it will not help you remember dates, names or other poems. Practice has effect only on the material practiced. To train your memory, try to develop the processes, requisite skills and attitude discussed above.

The mental muscles identified in Chapter 3 - Perception, Attention, Endurance, Organization, Flexibility, Coordination, and Conscious Recall - comprise the underlying mechanisms that support memory. The exercises you have done to strengthen these muscles have enhanced your sensory acuity, powers of apprehension and concentration and language skills, and sharpened your ability to use spatial cues, temporal cues and association techniques to foster recall. Keep exercising.

AGE-RELATED ISSUES

There are normal age-related memory problems. It is unrealistic to deny it. Implicit memory doesn't weaken; you still remember how to ride a bike or deal cards. But transience becomes an obstacle as we age, i.e., facts do fade over time. In addition, recently learned matter may be elusive, and the ability to learn new information slows. However, if you make an effort to learn something well and you take your time, you are able to recall it as well as a younger person.

ABSENT-MINDEDNESS is another memory problem. It is likely you were thinking about something else and not focusing on where you parked the car in the lot. This means, of course, the location wasn't fully encoded.

BLOCKING, that frustrating inability to retrieve a name you know as well as your own, can result from similar information obstructing its recall. It may have been properly stored but now, thanks to overload, it is just beyond reach. Half of such memories are retrieved within a minute.

MISATTRIBUTION is when you may have the right memory, but the wrong source, time, place, or people. Part of the recollection is correct, but you may have forgotten where, when or how you originally knew it. Older memories are most affected by misattribution.

SUGGESTIBILITY is having a false memory based on something you heard or read. Oft-told family stories fall into this category. People say they aren't sure if they really remember the event or they heard about it so often, they think they "remember" it. Childhood friends may so vividly describe incidents involving you that you begin to have that "memory."

Suggestibility is a phenomenon seen in eye-witness reports. One person may say the suspect was wearing a blue jacket. Other witnesses "remember" a blue jacket, too, or at least think they do.

PHYSICAL IMPEDIMENTS to memory include head trauma, heredity, poor vision, poor hearing, illness, injury, inactivity, and fatigue.

MENTAL OBSTACLES comprise dementia, depression, hypertension, stress, inattention, interference, distractions, disorganization, and medications.

FUNCTIONAL PROBLEMS stem from not making and using association-prompting cues.

MEMORY'S ENEMIES

Alcohol	Inattention
Poor Nutrition	Interference
Poor Vision, Hearing	Distractions
Inactivity	Disorganization
Fatigue	Not Using Cues

STRATEGIES

❖ The best way to overcome memory's enemies is to PAY ATTENTION to what you want to remember.

❖ When you need to learn something, focus, concentrate. Remove *all* distractions, including radio and TV.

❖ If content is important, write it down. If necessary, keep repeating it until you can write it. Speaking and writing reinforce memory.

❖ Consciously do what your brain does automatically: Associate new material with what you already know. Unusual associations are more memorable.

❖ To retrieve material, mentally recreate situations. Think back to your last contact with it. Use the spatial cues noted above. Push your brain to search for clues and links that will help you remember.

❖ Don't try to do too much at once or at the last minute. Rushing makes you forget. When going out, anticipate what you will need to take with you. Give yourself enough lead-in time to assemble the items.

❖ Be prepared. If you are going to be among a group of people, go over names of those who might be there. Anticipate discussions: Refresh your recollection of movies, books, programs, events, current affairs, names in the news, etc.

❖ Get organized. Your mother was right; everything does have a place. Get into the habit of putting it back there.

❖ Use calendars, appointment books, lists. Keep records. Take notes. Leave reminders for yourself.

❖ When something is on the tip of your tongue, relax. Stop thinking about it. It will surface - sooner or later.

TECHNIQUES

Mnemonic devices are techniques specifically designed to help you remember. They are helpful, effective and efficient. It is clever, not a sign of weakness, to use them. Two excellent mnemonics, Memory Pegs and Rhyme Schemes, are described below. Learn and utilize them. Make up your own devices.

MEMORY PEGS: Visualize a familiar room in detail. Select features in it to serve as Memory Pegs - chair, bed, doorknob, hook, lamp, switch, cabinet, desk, etc. At first, choose 4-6 items to remember, and virtually "hang" each item on a Peg. The more unusual the peg-item image, the easier it will be to remember. To recall your list, visualize the room again and "see" yourself lift each item from its hook.

Begin to use this effective technique as soon as you feel comfortable with it. It is worth the effort; it works. Increase the number of items to be pegged as you become more proficient.

RHYME SCHEME: Rhyme each number from 1-10 with a simple word, e.g., One-Sun, Two-Shoe, Three-Tree, Four-Door, Five-Hive, Six-Sticks, Seven-Heaven, Eight Gate, Nine-Wine, Ten-Hen (or make up your own rhymes). You won't forget these simple key words; just saying the numbers brings them to mind.

Let's say you want to get a newspaper, return books to the library, buy milk, juice, apples and coffee, leave your boots to be heeled, pick up clothes at the cleaners, go to the post office, and meet a friend. You might do it this way: See the newspaper in flames ignited by the heat of the sun; books wearing shoes; milk coming out of a cow straddling a tree limb; yourself getting drenched by juice when you open the refrigerator door; apples getting stung by bees swarming out of a hive; a coffee can being beaten by sticks; winged, haloed angels trudging in your boots; clothes swinging on the garden gate; stamps pouring out of the wine bottle into your stemmed glass; and your friend wearing a clucking chicken as a hat. It isn't hard to remember outlandish pictures you paint for yourself.

Create Your Own: Compose mnemonics to meet your personal needs. Use acronyms, initials of what you want to remember, e.g., ROYGBIV, the colors of the rainbow, abbreviations or concoct a system.

Let's say you want to remember the difference between annual and perennial flowers. The former live one season;

the latter return every year. Deliberately tell yourself the "p" in perennials is closer in the alphabet to "y" for yearly, or the "a" in annuals is number one in the alphabet, so annuals bloom one time. Links you forge yourself are especially strong.

Memory may be complicated, but it can and should be aided, trained and strengthened.

AGE SMART

MENTAL FITNESS WORKOUT
7

RELAXATION WARM-UP
Follow the directions on Page 11.

MENTAL CALISTHENICS
C 7a Say the months of the year out loud in correct order; now say them in reverse order; now in alphabetical order.

C 7b Calculate the sum of the numbers in your birthday, xx/xx/xxxx; your phone number, including area code. Repeat this exercise whenever you have time with other birthdays and phone numbers you know.

SENSORY DRILLS
A 7a Whenever you answer the phone, try to identify the speaker before s/he says who it is. Try to identify voices you hear on radio, TV, movies before seeing or learning who the person is.

O 7b Try to recognize fragrances - perfumes, lotions, crèmes, soaps - to the point where you can identify them by odor, not labels.

I 7 Observe the letters displayed below for √45, √√30, √√√15 seconds.

1) Imagine covering the letters with the grid below it. Which letters would you be able to see in the circles? The letter T is shown as an example. Write the letters which would be visible in the other circles in your MFJ.

3) In less than √60, √√45, √√√30 seconds, write the word that can be made from those letters.

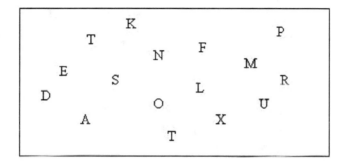

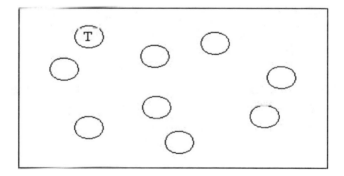

VISUALIZATION

Vs 7 Illustrate a story of something that happened to you or someone you know.

SPRINTS

Sp 7 Name as many uniforms as you can in 30 seconds.

MENTAL GYMNASTICS

MENTAL GYMNASTICS

MG 7 Correctly read the following un-spaced passages:

√

IthasbeenfivedayssinceIleftLondon. – *DanielMason*

Nothingsorevolutionaryhadhappenedsincetheyear300.
– *HenryAdams*

Wearecreaturesofoutsideinfluences;asarulewedonotthink,
weonlyimitate. – *MarkTwain*

√√

Onreflection,theseconclusionsarepreciselywhatonewouldex
pectifasociety'sinnovativenessisdeterminedbymanyindepen
dentfactors. – *JaredDiamond*

Alogiccanbemadeoutofanything;itliesnotinthetruthorfalsity
ofanidea,butinthemeansofitspracticalapplication.
– *NadineGordimer*

Fromthegreatlimbofamightyoakhungacoupleofcrudetorche
softhesortthatcarinspectorsthrustunderPullmancarswhena
trainpullsinatnight, – *H.L.Mencken*

√√√

Infact,ifyoucouldforgetmortality,andthatusedtobeeasierhere
thaninmostplaces,youcouldreallybelievethattimeiscircular,a
ndnotlinearandprogressiveasourcultureisbentonproving.
– *WallaceStegner*

Workingonachallengingjob,ridingthecrestofatremedouswa
ve,andteachingone'schildthelettersofthealphabetarethekin
dofexperiencesthatfocusourwholebeinginaharmoniousrus
hofenergyandliftusoutoftheanxietiesandboredomthatchar
acterizesomuchofeverydaylife. – *MihalyCsikszentmihalyi*

Inthedarknessspirithandswerefelttoflutterandwhenprayerb
ymantrashadbeendirectedtotheproperquarterafaintbutincr
easingluminosityofrubylightbecamegraduallyvisible,theapp
aritionoftheethericdoublebeingparticularlylifelikeowingtoth
edischargeofvividraysfromthecrownoftheheadandface.
– *JamesJoyce*

RESISTANCE TRAINING

RT 7 In your MFJ, alphabetize the words in the following paragraph:

"Sometimes it is very hard to pay attention to a speaker when there's a lot of activity going on around you. At the last meeting I attended, so many people were talking, getting up, leaving their places and ignoring the program, committee members became incensed."

MENTAL AEROBICS

MA 7 Study the paired words in column A until you think you know them.

Cover column A. In your MFJ, copy column B and write the correct match to each word. Check your work.

After B is accurate, repeat with column C, keeping A and B covered until you are finished

Repeat the exercise until you correctly associate all the words in the √, √√, √√√ group you are attempting. Good short-term memory practice.

√

A	B	C
Metal – Wood	Orange	Tears
Orange – Apricot	Skate	Wood
Baby – Tears	Fire	Girl
Sky – Earth	Baby	Apricot
Skate – Girl	Sky	Quilt
Fire – Quilt	Metal	Earth

√√

A	B	C
Rose – Flower	Piano	Eagle
Floor – Ring	Rose	Mouse
High – Low	Basket	Book
Lion – Eagle	Low	Cow
Egg – Chicken	Elbow	Dictionary
Cow – Bread	Egg	Ring
Basket – Chimney	Frame	Chimney
Elbow – Mouse	Lion	Flower
Frame – Book	Bread	Chicken
Piano – Dictionary	Floor	High

√√√

A	B	C
Black – White	Lamp	Ocean
Doll – Carriage	Canoe	Tomato
Floor – Broom	Airplane	Flag
Canoe – Green	Artist	Opposite
Ocean – Tree	Vacant	Pilot
Airplane – Snow	Telephone	Onion
Fast – Slow	Fast	Snow
Can – Telephone	Ruler	Can
Opposite – Tall	White	Truck
Truck – Vacant	Tree	Plant
Flag – Dog	Tall	Carriage
Ruler – Tomato	Dog	Slow
Pilot – card	Doll	Green
Artist – Plant	Card	Floor
Lamp – Onion	Broom	Black

WEIGHT LIFTING

WL 7 Answer the following questions in your MFJ.
a. According to the United States Constitution, if the vice-president dies, who would be president?
b. If four days ago was the day before Sunday, what will the day after tomorrow be?

c. Water lilies double every 24 hours. At the beginning of the summer there was one lily on a lovely lake. It took 60 days to cover the lake with lilies. On what day was the lake half covered?

STRETCHING

St 7 Make up nicknames for your friends and family. Explain your choices.

CONSCIOUS RECALL

CR 7 Describe in detail your most vivid memory.

COOL DOWN

Reread your MFJ entries – goals, exercises, observations, log. Think about the progress you've made toward your goals. How might you do better? Analyze your answer carefully. Record a new set of goals in your MFJ. Use them as criteria to judge your progress as you *AGE SMART* successfully.

Your Aging IQ Correct Answers

1. T	6. F
2. T	7. T
3. F	8. T
4. F	9. T
5. T	10. T

No wise person ever wished to be younger.
Jonathan Swift

8

THE AGE SMART
FITNESS FINALS

Congratulations. You made it to the Finals. The challenges below will keep you on your mental toes and help you maintain your mental fitness.

Try to do a *MFW* Fitness Finals set each week. A set consists of one exercise from each category - Calisthenics, Sensory Drills, Isometrics, Visualization, Sprints, Mental Gymnastics, Resistance Training, Mental Aerobics, Weight Lifting, Stretching, and Conscious Recall.

There are approximately eight exercises in each area, with enough variations and possible adaptations to engage you for several months. When you have completed the Fitness Finals, repeat any *MFW* or any *Age Smart* exercise. Enough time will have elapsed for the challenge to have returned. Remember to enter all responses in your Mental Fitness Journal.

Begin each workout with the Relaxation Warm-up you've used in each *MFW*. End with a Cool Down in which you consider your status and progress. Reflecting will engage your self-image and problem solving skills and deepen your commitment.

Identify areas where you see Mental Fitness advancement. Identify Mental Fitness Functions you still need to work on. Keep an anecdotal record in your MFJ.

HAVE FUN!

AGE SMART. AGE WELL. STAY FIT. BE HAPPY.

AGE SMART

MENTAL FITNESS WORKOUT # 8

RELAXATION WARM-UP
Follow directions on Page 11.

MENTAL CALISTHENICS
Alternate between numerical and word calisthenics when you do your *MFWs*. Don't forget - you can do most calisthenics anytime, anywhere, whenever you have a few minutes. Try to give yourself mini-mental-massages frequently.

1. Count aloud as quickly as possible.

    Up by 2, down by 2
    2, 4, 6, 8, 10 ...100
    100, 98, 96, 94, 92 ... 2

    Next time   Up by 3, down by 3
    3, 6, 9, 12, 1 5 ..99
    100, 97, 94, 91, 88 ... 1

    Next time by 4, then 5, etc. Try to get up to 10.

2. Attach an object to each letter in the alphabet: A-airplane, B-bottle, C-chalk.... Next time you do this exercise, attach two objects to each letter: A-apple, alabaster; B-box, bike.... Work up to five objects at a time for each letter. Try to think of different objects each round. This is an excellent anytime, anywhere mini-mental-massage.

3. Say pairs of non-sequential multiplication tables aloud as quickly as possible, alternating between them. For example, the 1 and 12 tables:

1x1=1, 12x1=12; 1x2=2, 12x2=24...1x12=12, 12x12=144.

When you repeat this exercise, use different alternating non-sequential pairs, e.g., 2 and 7, 3 and 10, 4 and 9, or any non-sequential combination you choose.

4. Practice mental division. Make up your own examples using products from the above exercise.
5. Say each tongue twister four times aloud, as quickly as you can.
    a. Lovely lemon liniment.
    b. Betty better butter Brad's bread.
    c. We surely shall see the sun shine soon.
    d. Selfish shellfish.
    e. Girl gargoyle, guy gargoyle.
    f. Tie twine to three tree twigs.
6. Read a paragraph aloud omitting every third word; next time, every fifth word; then every tenth word.
7. Recite (don't sing) the words to your favorite song; to the Star Spangled Banner; to any song you know.
8. Repeat each tongue twister twice, as quickly as you can.
    a. I saw Esau kissing Kate. I saw Esau, he saw me, and she saw I saw Esau.
    b. One-One was a racehorse. Two-two was one, too. When One-One won one race, Two-Two won one, too.

SENSORY DRILLS

1. Choose a simple object on your desk, dresser or table. Study it carefully. When you think you know it well, cover it, and write a detailed description. Include size, color, condition, purpose, features, appearance, attractions, etc. Repeat this exercise until you can write an accurate, detailed description without looking.
2. Ask someone to hand you objects while your eyes are closed. Try to correctly identify each object. Record the objects and time it takes you to get it right. Repeat this exercise with other objects. See

if you can increase your accuracy as you decrease the time.

3. Become familiar with distinctive odors of fruits and vegetables, e.g., cilantro, garlic, parsley, citrus, bananas, until you can identify them with your eyes closed by smell alone.

4. In a fairly noisy place, try to correctly identify all the sounds you hear in five minutes. Do this exercise another time in a pet store. In the Mall. In a playground. In a quiet place.

5. Try to identify different juices, sodas, teas, etc. only by their tastes. Ask someone to pour, and drink with your eyes closed.

6. Choose a vowel sound - long ā, short ĕ, etc. For five minutes, listen for words containing the sound. Listen to the radio, TV, people around you. List the words you hear with the sound you've chosen. As you gain proficiency, increase the length of time you listen for the sound. This will really hone your listening skills.

7. Select your clothes and get dressed without opening your eyes. Describe your (interesting?) outfit in your MFJ. Tell how you felt doing all this without being able to see.

8. Play "I Spy" with people of all ages. Choose an object within everyone's view. Say, "I spy with my little eye something that begins with ...." Tell the players only the first letter of the object. The game is as simple to play as it sounds, but it can be challenging. You'd be amazed at how little we notice unless we really try to be observant. It's also great to play on a car trip with kids.

ISOMETRICS

1. Copy a picture or draw an object with your non-dominant hand.

2. Write the alphabet with your non-dominant hand. Practice until you can do it in less than 15 seconds.

3. While you listen to music, let your dominant hand move a pencil randomly over a piece of paper in time to the selection. When the music ends, color the spaces you created.

   Next time, do this exercise holding the pencil in your non-dominant hand. Note any differences in your comfort level and in the drawings.

4. When you enter a store, a room, a restaurant, or auditorium, try to estimate the number of people in it; the number in front of you, to your right, your left, above you, behind you. It helps you to focus and get into the habit of becoming aware of your surroundings. Both practices aid memory. Monitor your estimates and keep at it until they are fairly accurate.

5. Estimate the number of lines in a paragraph in a book, a magazine, a newspaper, e.g., more than 12, less than 10, fewer than six. To sharpen your perception, repeat this exercise daily until your estimates are fairly accurate.

6. Use your non-dominant hand to brush your teeth.

7. Revise the usual order in which you do things. If you usually put stockings, socks, shoes on the right foot first, next time, put them on the left foot first. When you dress, put clothes on the "other" arm or leg first.

   Reverse the order in which you usually button shirts/blouses, i.e., top-to-bottom or *vice versa*. Use your non-dominant hand to do the buttoning.

   If convenient, make the bed from a different side. Prepare and eat breakfast with your non-dominant hand. It may feel awkward, but you'll create new synapses.

8. Get a new perspective. Sit in a different position at the family dining table. In what ways do things seem different?

VISUALIZATION

1. Choose an object for each of your initials. Visualize it, and write a detailed description - size, color, use, condition, purpose, value, etc. Use other people's initials. Do this exercise often to sharpen your powers of observation and focus your attention.

2. Next time you go marketing, try not to use your list. Instead, mentally group the items you need by department. Then visualize the store, the most efficient way of going through it and yourself putting the items in your basket. Start with 4-6 items. This is good training in organization, association and remembering.

3. Hang images of tasks you want to do on the memory pegs you established in Chapter 7.

4. Another time, visualize items or tasks in outlandish images using the number-rhyme scheme you created in Chapter 7.

5. Visualize a table set for a formal dinner. Describe a place setting.

6. Visualize and describe the front and back of a penny, a nickel, a dime, a quarter. Repeat this exercise until your descriptions are accurate.

7. Visualize a map of the United States. Accurately name the 48 contiguous states starting in the NE, next time the SW, then the SE, and finally the NW.

8. Use a sheet of graph paper for this exercise in spatial orientation. Draw a line following the directions. Be sure to start at a point that will permit you to execute all the moves without going off the paper. Draw the symbols shown at the indicated coordinates.

    √ East 4, North 11, East 11 •, South 4, West 9 ▲, South 11, East 4, North 8 ◊, East 6, South 10

    √√ West 5, South 6, West 5, North 9 □, West 14, South 4 #, East 5, North 2, East 3, South 12, West 6 •, South 4, East 15 ∞, North 3, East 7

√√√ South 5, West 3, South 6 ◊, East 11, North 7, East 12, South 15 □, West 17, North 4, West 5 ▲, South 16, East 3, North 9 ∩, East 5, South 11, East 5, North 11 ●, East 12, South 14, West 28 ◌

SPRINTS

1. Name as many different articles of clothing as you can in one minute.
2. Name as many fruits in 30 seconds as you can that can be eaten with the skin on.
3. Name as many colors as possible in one minute.
4. Name as many instruments used to hit balls in games as you can.
5. Name as many means of transportation as you can in two minutes.
6. Name as many animals as you can with fur in 30 seconds.
7. In 30 seconds, list as many words as you can that rhyme with sing; clown; break; run; hope; jump; hair; merry.
8. In 20 seconds, say as many words as you can that begin with the first letter of your first name, the last letter of your first name, the first and last letters of your last name. Use letters in the first and last names of family and friends each time you repeat this exercise.

MENTAL GYMNASTICS

1. Assign a word to each letter of your name and construct a meaningful phrase or sentence with them. Sample: JAMES - Just about midnight, Ellen sang.
2. Write all the *proper* nouns you can think of beginning with R, with the letters in PLAN, with those in your mother's maiden name, or your neighbor's first name, or the street you live on, or....
3. Be a word archeologist. In your MFJ, write the names of the hidden cities in the following words:

angriest, animal, diagnose, dottier, hasten, nerved, planes, reddens, testier

4. Word Pyramid. Start with the letters EN (the name of the letter or a printer's measure). On each line add a letter to the previous word, and rearrange the letters to make a new word. Try to reach a 6-letter word. Do all the work in your MFJ.

EN

_ _ _

_ _ _ _

_ _ _ _ _

_ _ _ _ _ _

To repeat this exercise, begin with any two letters at random.

5. Solve this code for quote and author. Each number represents the same letter throughout. A few clues are provided to help you get started.

6	8	3

6	8	2	1		6
				s	

17	19	6	3	1

8	17	10	10	2	4	3		
							s	s

2	
	s

4	3	15	3	1

3	20	6	2	4	9	18	2	
								s

8	3	13

2	4

6	8	3

8	3	17	1	6

5	19

16	17	4

25	3	17	4

25	17	26	27	18	3	
						s

1	5	18			3	17	18
			s	s			

6. Make up a conversation between an alien from outer space and a police officer; between a remote control and a TV set.
7. Think of as many first names as possible for each letter in the name of the town/city in which you were born.
8. Consecutively number every letter in the alphabet. Decode the following:
   25 15 21   4 15 14 20   12 9 22 5   9 14   1
   23 15 18 12 4   1 12 12   1 12 15 14 5

RESISTANCE TRAINING

1. See how many words you can make out of the letters in your full name. It's easier if you write in your MFJ.
2. Listen to a radio or TV news broadcast. Without taking notes, summarize the lead story. Work up to summarizing 5, 15, 30 minutes of news broadcasts.
3. See how many 3 , 4-, 5-, 6-letter words you can make in three minutes from the letters R G G I E N
4. Without looking at it, describe the front of a one dollar bill. (See how little we notice about objects we frequently handle.) Now study it carefully. Put it away and write a detailed description. Repeat this exercise until you can write a full and accurate description.
5. Verbally explain how to lace and tie a shoe without using objects, hand motions, illustrations or handling anything.
6. Name as many different kinds of games played with a ball as you can.
7. Agent 008, you have an assignment. You have to send a report to your supervisor conveying your sense of what is happening in a particular place at a particular time. Your contact needs to know about the people present - number, sex, approximate age, attire, actions - and your interpretation of what it all means.

For this report, choose a time and place where things are happening and several people are present. Work for √10,√√15,√√√20 minutes at the site you have chosen. Write a detailed description and analysis of all you observe.

8. Name as many countries on the continent of Africa as you can.

9. If you don't already know them, learn the names of the 50 United States, their symbols and capital cities. List the states in alphabetical order. Add their abbreviations and capital cities.

   Another time, list the capitals in alphabetical order. Add the state abbreviations.

MENTAL AEROBICS

1. Look at the scrambled words below. Without writing them down, try to unscramble them in less than three minutes. Write the word that doesn't belong in the group in your MFJ.

   A N G I E B O,   L I M G R O D A,   W O S R L E F N U,

   E P R A A N I L,   T A U N E I P,   N S A Y P

2. Spell a synonym of each of the words below backwards. Example: Automobile - rac

   Sky   Sad   Up   Dull   Fast   Add   Shout   Run

3. Choose a category, e.g., occupations, animals, countries, flowers, cities. Name something in the category for each letter of the alphabet, e.g., animals: A-aardvark, B-bear, C-cougar....

4. Write six sentences by combining appropriate words from each column below. The words that belong in each sentence are not in the same row. You will have to look through the columns to find them.

The capitalized words are an example. *The skilled tailor matched the fabrics artfully.*

Subject	Adjective	Verb	Noun	Adverb
dog	capable	studied	problem	ARTFULLY
author	SKILLED	discharged	customer	efficiently
TAILOR	watchful	assisted	assignments	satisfactorily
student	friendly	growled	FABRICS	rapidly
mechanic	diligent	wrote	yard	carefully
salesper-son	expert	completed	responsibili-ties	menacingly
assistant	prolific	MATCHED	drafts	assiduously

5. Practice creating mnemonics. Read a newspaper article. List the first √4, √√6, √√√8 names that appear in the article. Assign a word to the first or last initial in each name, and make up a sentence with the words to help you recall them. For example, George Bush, Dick Chaney, Harry Reid, and Nancy Pelosi - "Gee, chocolate's really powerful."

6. Create acronyms for items, places, people you want to remember.

7. Copy these words into your MFJ. Write the words they spell backwards.

    plug   top   smug   time   live   straw

8. See how many 4-letter and longer words you can find in "reincarnation" in two minutes.

WEIGHT LIFTING

1. Do these simple arithmetic problems as quickly as you can. Write the answers in you MFJ.

a.	9	-	5	=	8	+	8	=	3	+	6	=
b.	4	x	2	=	9	+	7	=	1	+	2	=
c.	12	-	6	=	7	x	9	=	8	x	4	=
d.	5	x	5	=	2	+	6	=	10	+	1	=
e.	3	+	6	=	11	-	5	=	7	+	6	=
f.	5	x	7	=	2	+	3	=	8	-	2	=
g.	6	x	3	=	4	-	1	=	12	-	5	=
h.	9	x	8	=	1	+	7	=	2	x	8	=
i.	15	-	8	=	4	x	9	=	3	+	9	=
j.	7	-	6	=	5	+	0	=	8	x	7	=

Make up, write your own simple arithmetic problems in your MFJ and do them. Solving them activates large areas in your brain.

2. Choose a sentence from a newspaper, a magazine, a book. Try to rearrange the words to form a different sentence.
3. Name as many animals as you can with claws, with antlers, with hooves, with horns.
4. Name four oceans, six rivers, five lakes.
5. Write as many words as you can think of that begin with the same first syllable as each of the following words: calendar, garden, fanfare, compare, mentor.
6. Unscramble the clue words. Write them in your MFJ. Rearrange the letters that would appear in the circles to form words to fit in the blank spaces shown beneath the words.

scuescs _ _ _ _ O_ _ _

tgnaemur _ _ O_ _ O_ _ _ _

pirchte O_ _ _ _ O_ _ O_

bouteasl _ _ O_ _ _ _ _ O_

taarepse _ _ O_ _ _ O_ O_ _

zylneaa O_ _ O_ _ O_ _ _

gihcpar O_ _ O_ _ _ _ _

_ _ _ _ _ _ _ _ _ _ _ _ _ _ _

7. Make up a story containing the words in each √, √√, √√√ group.

√   Trees - Violin · Couple - Duck - Musician - Abroad - Café - Birds - Roast - Outdoor

√√   Trees - Violin - Couple - Duck - Musician - Abroad - Café - Birds - Roast - Outdoor - Wine - Nest

√√√ Trees - Violin - Couple - Duck - Musician - Abroad - Café - Birds - Roast - Outdoor - Wine - Nest - France - Rice - Fountain

STRETCHING
1. Write a letter to an imaginary pen pal in a country you would like to visit.
2. Watch a play, movie or TV program you have never seen, and write a review.
3. Sit in front of a mirror and try to draw a self-portrait.
4. Take a day trip to a place you've never been.

5. Do a jigsaw puzzle.
6. Follow the pattern a a b b a, and complete this limerick: There once was a fellow named Mike, Who went for a ride on a bike.... Or write a limerick of your own
7. Use your non-dominant hand to write your name, address, phone number, and email address.
8. Do an activity you've never done before: Paint, bake, sculpt, cook, draw, quilt, build a bookcase, learn to swim, take a flying lesson. Try something you've always meant to do, but for whatever reason haven't gotten to yet.

CONSCIOUS RECALL

1. Memorize three names and numbers in your personal phone book each day. Repeat them cumulatively each time, i.e., first day memorize and repeat three, second day memorize three more and repeat all six, etc. Work up to five days, 15 names and numbers. Chunk numbers, make associations, visualize locations of numbers on the phone pad, etc. This practice will help strengthen your data storage techniques and ability.
2. Name $\sqrt{8}$, $\sqrt{\sqrt{10}}$, $\sqrt{\sqrt{\sqrt{12}}}$ objects you might use at the dinner table.
3. Name $\sqrt{8}$, $\sqrt{\sqrt{10}}$, $\sqrt{\sqrt{\sqrt{15}}}$ useful items found in or on a desk.
4. Whose picture is on the $1.00 bill? $5.00? $10.00? $20.00? $50.00? $100?
5. Sharpen your thinking and your geography. Write each capital city and match it with its country in your MFJ.

√	√√	√√√
London	Lisbon	Bern
Madrid	Athens	Rabat
Brussels	Berlin	Tehran
Rome	Cairo	Brasilia
Washington	Baghda	Vienna
Ottawa	Ankara	Prague
Copenhagen	Moscow	Havana
	Cape Town	Jerusalem
		Lima
		Beijing

6. Consciously recall personal data and record the information in your MFJ: The birthdays of your parents, siblings, spouse, children, children's spouses, and grandchildren; your wedding anniversary; children's wedding anniversaries.

7. Consciously recall professional data and enter the information in you MFJ: Your high school, year of graduation; college, degree, year of graduation; graduate school, degree, year of graduation; Work history - dates, employers, position/s held, names of colleagues, supervisors.

8. List what you ate for breakfast yesterday. Describe your sense memories. Tell how the foods looked, felt in your mouth, smelled, and tasted.

9. In your MFJ, name the last five books you read; the last five movies you saw; the last five plays, concerts, museums you attended; the last five people you spoke to on the phone.

AGE SMART
MENTAL FITNESS WORKOUT ANSWERS

Some exercises ask you to give as many responses to a prompt as you can. The answers provided below are just a few possible choices. You may think of many others.

MENTAL FITNESS WORKOUT #1

<u>MC 1b</u> There are 11 printed letters with curved lines: B C D G J O P Q R S U

<u>I 1</u>   There are 30 squares

<u>Sp 1</u>   *Musical Instruments:* Accordion, Bass, Bassoon, Bell, Castanets, Cello, Clarinet, Cornet, Drums, Dulcimer, English Horn, Flugelhorn, Flute, French Horn, Guitar, Harmonica, Harp, Hurdy-gurdy, Lute, Lyre, Oboe, Ocarina, Piano, Rattle, Recorder, Saxophone, Tambourine, Trombone, Trumpet, Tuba, Ukulele, Violin, Viola, Xylophone, Zither

<u>MA 1</u>   Roots, Pen, File, Case, Scales, Wings

<u>WL 1</u> √ *Waste not want not.* If you don't squander it (whatever *it* is), you'll have it when you need it.

Money is the root of all evil. Money causes problems. The original adage is *The love of money* is the root of all evil.

A rolling stone gathers no moss. It once was derogatory - moving around too much prevented a person from settling down, establishing roots, becoming responsible. Now it's used to compliment someone who's up on the latest.

√√ *A stitch in time saves nine.* Don't procrastinate.

Laugh and the world laughs with you, cry and you cry alone. People will like you better, you'll have more friends if you put on a happy face.

√√√ *He who laughs last, laughs best.* Don't let others' opinions stop you; when you succeed and prove them wrong, the last (best) laugh will be yours.

All that glitters is not gold. You can't tell a book by its cover. Both adages tell you appearances can be deceiving.

MENTAL FITNESS WORKOUT #2

<u>MC 2a</u> Argentina; Goat; Orange; Silver; Elm; Acura; Rottweiler; Shirt - or your choices

<u>I 2</u> The heart, # 8, does not appear.

<u>Sp 2</u> <u>*Countries in South America*</u> Argentina, Bolivia, Brazil, Chile, Colombia, Ecuador, French Guiana, Guyana, Paraguay, Peru, Suriname, Uruguay, Venezuela

<u>MA 2</u> √ <u>Flowers</u>: tulip, gladiola, rose, iris
<u>Professions</u>: instructor, lawyer, pharmacist, doctor
<u>Business Related</u>: agenda, notepad, file, minutes

√√ <u>Animals</u>: dog, tiger, elephant, squirrel
<u>Tools</u>: hammer, pliers, screwdriver, wrench
<u>Drinks</u>: wine, martini, water, lemonade
<u>Occupations</u>: architect, electrician, nurse, photographer

√√√ <u>Music</u>: violin, accordion, flute, guitar, piano
<u>Sports</u>: tennis, football, basketball, gymnastics
<u>Games</u>: checkers, bridge, chess, backgammon
<u>Jewelry</u>: necklace, ring, brooch, bracelet, tiara
<u>Furniture</u>: chair, footstool, couch, bed, table, credenza

<u>WL 2</u> The first multiplication example is 714 times 12; the second is 634 times 453.

MENTAL FITNESS WORKOUT #3

<u>MC 3b</u> *3, 8, 13, 18, 23, 28, 30, 31, 32, 33, 34, 35, 36, 37, 38, 39, 43, 48, 53, 58, 63, 68, 73, 78, 80, 81, 82, 83, 84, 85, 86, 87, 88, 89, 93, 98*

<u>I 3</u> There are five different kinds of arrows. They appear in rows arranged in reverse order on either side of the suns.

Sp 3   *Kitchen Items*: Tables, chairs, place mats, table cloths, refrigerator, oven, stove, micro-wave, sinks carving boards, cabinets, pantries, scales, food processors, can openers, toasters, toaster-ovens, dish drains, canisters, peelers, scrapers, gadgets, cutlery, dishes, glasses, jars, bowls

MG 3   The countries are Canada, Poland, Norway, Cyprus, Mexico, Turkey, Brazil, Sweden, Israel, France

MA 3   √ Being entirely honest with oneself is a good exercise. *Sigmund Freud*

There is no substitute for hard work. *Thomas Edison*

√√ But in science the credit goes to the man who convinces the world, not to the man to whom the idea first occurs. *Sir Francis Darwin*

The highest and best form of efficiency is the spontaneous cooperation of a free people. *Woodrow Wilson*

√√√ For instance, there is the kind of seriousness whose trademark is anguish, cruelty, derangement. *Susan Sontag*

Modern war is so expensive that we feel trade to be a better venue to plunder.... Showing war's irrationality and horror is of no effect upon him. The horrors make the fascination. *William James*

It is very difficult so difficult that it always has been difficult but even more difficult now to know what is the relation of human nature to the human mind because one has to know what is the relation of the act of creation to the subject the creator uses to create that thing. *Gertrude Stein*

WL 3 APPLAUSE

MENTAL FITNESS WORKOUT #4

Sp 4 *Head Coverings*: Baseball Cap, Bonnet, Cloche, Fedora, Golf Cap, Hat, Head Band, Helmut, Kerchief, Military Hat, Nurse Cap, Picture Hat, Scarf, Ski Hat, Skull Cap, Sleeping Cap, Snood, Stetson, Straw Hat, Surgical Cap, Swim Cap, Tennis Hat, Turban, Veil, Watch Cap, Wig

MG 4 No one said you had to stay within the circles. Get out of the box.

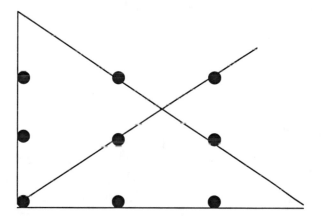

MA 4 His, Has, She; Fur, Run Cur, Rut; Bet, Let, Set, Tea, Ten Net; Man, Men; Bar, Bat, Bad, Bam , Ban, Nab; Sad, Sod, Dos, Dis; Imp, Mix, Him, Rim; Pat, Pet, Pit, Pot, Put, Tap, Tip, Top; Oar, Oat.

St 4 *Time Capsule Items:* Sheet music for *Let Me Call You Sweetheart*; One of the stolen Crown Jewels; Brownie Camera; First Oklahoma State Flag; Orville Wright's silk scarf; Costume from Serge Diaghilev's Ballets Russes and program signed by him, Nijinsky, Stravinsky, and Picasso; Ostrich Feather Hat; Phonograph Record; Fragment from San Francisco

Earthquake; Kathryn Hepburn's, Rachel Carson's, and Louis Armstrong's Baby Shoes; Letters between Jung and Freud; Cover of Good Housekeeping Magazine @ $1.00

CR 4 *First Five Presidents:* George Washington, John Adams, Thomas Jefferson, James Madison, James Monroe
Last Five Presidents: George W. Bush, William J. Clinton, George H. W. Bush, Ronald Reagan, Jimmy Carter

MENTAL FITNESS WORKOUT #5

<u>I 5</u>

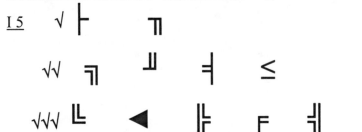

MG 5 The uncommon number is 276. The common feature in the other numbers is that the sum of the first and third digits equals the middle figure.

WL 5 √ Alien, Angry, Blast, Spoil, Miner, Craft
√√ Single, Normal, Thrive, Cavort, Tangle, Tremor, Season, Satisfy
√√√ Terrible, Conclude, Practical, Admirable, Harmonious, Atmosphere, Impossible, Inclination, Tentatively, Withholding

MENTAL FITNESS WORKOUT #6

<u>MC 6a</u> Monday, Tuesday, Wednesday, Thursday, Friday, Saturday, Sunday
yadnoM, yadseuT, yadsendeW, yadsruhT, yadirF, yadrutaS, yadnuS
Friday, Monday, Saturday, Sunday, Thursday, Tuesday, Wednesday

I 6   Place circles 7 and 10 on either side of 2 and 3. Put 1 on top of 8 and 9.

Sp 6   *Useful Tools:* Adz, Augur, Awl, Ax, Bench Vise, Chisels, Crow Bar, Drills and Bits, Files, Guns, Hammers, Jacks, Level, Nail Punch, Paint Scraper, Pick Ax, Plane, Pliers, Plumb Line, Punch, Putty Knife, Rooter, Rule, Sanders, Saws, Screed, Screw Drivers, Soldering Iron, Tape Measure, Trowel, Wire Stripper, Wire Cutter, Wrenches

MG 6   Architect, Comprehensive

RT 6   KCALB, THGIL, ROOLF, THGIN, DOOG, LLAT, YPPAH, LLAMS/ELTTIL, YTTERP, NEVE

MA 6   LIVING MATTER; *Animal; Vegetable;* <u>Dog</u>, Terrier, Collie; <u>Bird</u>, Wren, Canary; <u>Fruit</u>, Pear, Apple; <u>Flower</u>, Rose, Daisy

MENTAL FITNESS WORKOUT #7

MC 7a   January, February. March, April, May, June, July, August, September, October, November, December

December, November, October, September, August, July, June, May, April, March, February, January

April, August, December, February, January, July, June, March, May, November, October, September

I 7   Fortunate

Sp 7   *Uniforms:* Ambulance Workers, Cheerleaders, Cleaners, Doctors, EMTs, Fire Fighters, Lab Coats, Law Enforcement, Martial Arts, Military, Nurses, Postal Workers, Restaurant, Scouts, School, Sports, Work

MG 7   √ It has been five days since I left London. *Daniel Mason*

Nothing revolutionary had happened since the year 300. *Henry Adams*

We are creatures of outside influences; as a rule we do not think, we only imitate. *Mark Twain*

√√ On reflection, these conclusions are precisely what one would expect if a society's innovativeness is determined by many independent factors. *Jared Diamond*

A logic can be made out of anything; it lies not in the truth or falsity of an idea, but in the means of its practical application. *Nadine Gordimer*

From the great limb of a mighty oak hung a couple of crude torches of the sort that car inspectors thrust under Pullman cars when a train pulls in at night. *H.L. Menken*

√√√ In fact if you could forget mortality, and that used to be easier here than in most places, you could really believe that time is circular, and not linear and progressive as our culture is bent on proving. *Wallace Stegner*

Working on a challenging job, riding the crest of a tremendous wave, and teaching one's child the letters of the alphabet are the kinds of experiences that focus our whole being in a harmonious rush of energy and lift us out of the anxieties and boredom that characterize so much of every day life. *Mihaly Csikszentmihalyi*

In the darkness spirit hands were felt to flutter and when prayer by mantras had been directed to the proper quarter a faint but increasing luminosity of ruby light became gradually visible, the apparition of the etheric double being particularly lifelike owing to the discharge of vivid rays from the crown of the head and face. *James Joyce*

RT 7   a, activity, and, around, at, attended, attention, became, committee, getting, going, hard, I, ignoring, incensed, is, it, last, leaving, lot, many, meeting, members, of, on, pay, people, places, program, so, sometimes, speaker, talking, the, their, there's, to, up, very, were, when, you

WL 7   a. The president   b. Friday   c. 59

MENTAL FITNESS WORKOUT #8
The Fitness Finals!

SPRINTS

1. *Clothing Articles* Bathing Suit, Blouse, Boots, Clogs, Coat, Dress, Gown, Hat, Jacket, Jeans, Nightgown, Pajamas, Rainwear, Robe, Sandals, Shirt, Shoes, Skirt, Ski Suit, Slacks, Slippers, Socks, Snowsuit, Stockings, Suit, Sweater, Tuxedo

2. Fruits *Eaten with Skin* Apples, Apricots, Berries, Cherries, Dates, Figs, Grapes, Nectarines, Peaches, Pears, Plums, Prunes, Raisins

3. *Colors - Including any tint or shade you name of* Aqua, Beige, Black, Blue, Brown, Gold, Gray, Green, Mauve, Maroon, Orange, Pink, Purple, Red, Silver,

4. *Instruments Used to Propel Balls in Games* Bat, Racket, Hand, Foot, Paddle, Head, Mallet, Stick, Club, The Crosse

5. *Means of Transportation* Airplane, Bicycle, Boat, Bus, Cab, Cable Car, Camel, Canoe, Car, Carriage, Coach, Elephant, Foot, Horse, Hot Air Balloon, Ice Skates, Inline Skates, Motorbike, Motorcycle, Raft, Railroad Train, Roller Skates, Row Boat, Sailboat, Scooter, Skateboard, Skiff, Skis, Sleigh, Snow Board, Steamship, Subway, SUV, Taxi, Tricycle, Tram, Trolley, Truck, Unicycle, Van, Zeppelin,

6. *Animals with Fur* Badger, Beaver, Bear, Bobcat Chinchilla, Coyote, Coypu (Nutria), Fisher (Marten), Fox, Lynx, Marmot, Mink, Muskrat, Otter, Ocelot, Opossum, Polecat, Rabbit, Raccoon, Sable, Skunk, Squirrel, Weasel (Ermine), Wolf, Wolverine

MENTAL GYMNASTICS

3. Tangiers, Manila, San Diego, Detroit, Athens, Denver, Naples, Dresden, Trieste

4. *Word Pyramid:* En, End, Send, Dense, Sender,

5. The thirst after happiness is never extinguished in the heart of man. Jean Jacques Rousseau

8. You don't live in a world all alone.

RESISTANCE TRAINING

3. Egg, Erg, Gig, Gin, Ire, Rig, Grin, Rein, Ring, Reign, Ginger

5. A My Name is..., Baseball, Basketball, Bowling, Box Ball, Cricket, Croquet, Dodge Ball, Football, Hand Ball, Jacks, Polo, Slug, Soccer, Softball, Tennis, Volley Ball, Water Polo,

7. <u>*Countries in Africa*</u> Algeria, Angola, Benin, Botswana, Burkina Faso, Burundi, Cameroon, Central African Rep., Chad, Congo, Dem. Rep. Congo (Zaire), Djibouti, Egypt, Equatorial Guinea, Eritrea, Ethiopia, Gabon, Gambia, Ghana, Guinea Bissau, Guinea, Ivory Coast, Kenya, Lesotho, Liberia, Libya, Malawi, Mali, Mauritania, Morocco, Mozambique, Namibia, Niger, Nigeria, Rwanda, Senegal, Sierra Leone, Somalia, South Africa, Sudan, Swaziland, Tanzania, Togo, Tunisia, Uganda, Zambia, Zimbabwe

8. <u>*States, Capitals, Abbreviations*</u>

States, Capitals, Abbreviations

AL	Alabama	Montgomery	MT	Montana	Helena
AK	Alaska	Juneau	NE	Nebraska	Lincoln
AZ	Arizona	Phoenix	NV	Nevada	Carson City
AR	Arkansas	Little Rock	NH	New Hampshire	Concord
CA	California	Sacramento	NJ	New Jersey	Trenton
CO	Colorado	Denver	NM	New Mexico	Santa Fe
CT	Connecticut	Hartford	NY	New York	Albany
DE	Delaware	Dover	NC	North Carolina	Raleigh
FL	Florida	Tallahassee	ND	North Dakota	Bismarck
GA	Georgia	Atlanta	OH	Ohio	Columbus
HA	Hawaii	Honolulu	OK	Oklahoma	Oklahoma City
ID	Idaho	Boise	OR	Oregon	Salem
IL	Illinois	Springfield	PA	Pennsyl-vania	Harrisburg
IN	Indiana	Indianapolis	RI	Rhode Island	Providence
IA	Iowa	Des Moines	SC	South Carolina	Columbia
KS	Kansas	Topeka	SD	South Dakota	Pierre
KY	Kentucky	Frankfort	TN	Tennessee	Nashville
LA	Louisiana	Baton Rouge	TX	Texas	Austin
ME	Maine	Augusta	UT	Utah	Salt Lake City
MD	Maryland	Annapolis	VT	Vermont	Montpelier
MA	Massachu-setts	Boston	VA	Virginia	Richmond
MI	Michigan	Lansing	WA	Washington	Olympia
MN	Minnesota	St. Paul	WV	West Virginia	Charleston
MS	Mississippi	Jackson	WI	Wisconsin	Madison
MO	Missouri	Jefferson City	WY	Wyoming	Cheyenne

State Capitals and Abbreviations

Albany	NY	Dover	DE	Oklahoma City	OK
Annapolis	MD	Frankfort	KY	Olympia	WA
Atlanta	GA	Hartford	CT	Phoenix	AZ
Augusta	ME	Harrisburg	PA	Pierre	SD
Austin	TX	Helena	MT	Providence	RI
Baton Rouge	LA	Honolulu	HA	Raleigh	NC
Bismarck	ND	Indianapolis	IN	Richmond	VA
Boise	ID	Jackson	MS	Sacramento	CA
Boston	MA	Jefferson City	MO	Salem	OR
Carson City	NV	Juneau	AK	Salt Lake City	UT
Charleston	WV	Lansing	MI	Santa Fe	NM
Cheyenne	WY	Lincoln	NE	Springfield	IL
Columbia	SC	Little Rock	AR	St. Paul	MN
Columbus	OH	Madison	WI	Tallahassee	FL
Concord	NH	Montgomery	AL	Topeka	KS
Des Moines	IA	Montpelier	VT	Trenton	NJ
Denver	CO	Nashville	TN		

MENTAL AEROBICS

1. Begonia, Marigold, Sunflower, Petunia, Pansy. Airplane doesn't belong in the group.
2. Sky - snevaeh; Sad - yppahnu; Up - evoba; Dull - gnirob; Fast - kciuq; Add - latot; Shout - lley; Run - evom ylkciuq/etarepo
4. The watchful dog growled menacingly in the yard.
The prolific author wrote drafts assiduously.
The diligent student completed his assignments carefully.
The expert mechanic solved the problem rapidly.
The friendly salesperson assisted the customer satisfactorily.
The capable assistant discharged her responsibilities efficiently.

7. Gulp, Pot, Gum, Emit, Evil, Warts
8. These are some of the more than 290 words you could find in "Reincarnation": race, racer, rain, raincoat, rainier, ran, rancor, rant, rare, rate, rater, ratio, ration, react, reaction, rear, recant, rein, reincarnation, rent, rice, ricer, riot, rite, roar, rote, earn, enact, erotic, errant, icier, icon, inaction, inane, incarnate, incarnation, incinerator, incite, inert, inertia, inner, innocent, interior, intern, into, iota, iron, ironic, narrate, narration, nation, near, neat, nectar, neon, nice, nicer, nicotine, nine, none, note, notice, cane, canine, canny, cannot, canoe, canon, canter, carat, care, carnation, carrot, cart, carton, cater, cent, certain, cite, coat, coin, cone, contain, container, core, corn, cornea, corner, crane, crate, creation, creator, criteria, criterion, crone, acne, acorn, acre, action, actor, aerate, airier, ancient, anoint, anon, antenna, antic, aorta, arcane, area, arena, taco, tanner, tannic, taro, tear, tenor, terrain, tiara, tier, tine, tire, tone, tonic, tore, torn, trace, tracer, train, trainer, trance, trice, trio, ocean, octane, once, orate, orca, orient, ornate

WEIGHT LIFTING

1. a) 4,16,9 b) 8,16,3 c) 6,63,32 d) 25,8,11 e) 9,6,13 f) 35,5,6 g) 18,3,7 h) 72,8,16 i) 7,36,12 j) 1,5,56
3. *Claws* Dog, Bear, Ape, Monkey, Lemur, Cat Family, Bat, Beaver, Crab, Anteater, Sloth, Armadillo *Antlers* Deer, Elk, Moose *Hooves* Swine, Deer, Antelope, Horse, Zebra, Camel, Bison, Water Buffalo, Yak, Rhinoceros *Horns* Cattle, Bison, Sheep, Goats
4. *Oceans* World (Antarctic), Atlantic, Indian, Southern, Pacific *Rivers* Amazon, Elbe, Hudson, Mississippi, Missouri, Nile, Seine, Thames, Yangtze *Lakes* Caspian Sea (Europe/Asia) Largest by area and volume; Lake Baikal (Siberia) Deepest, largest freshwater by volume; Dead Sea (Israel) Lowest; Lake Superior (U.S.) Largest freshwater by surface

area; The Great Lakes (U.S.) Huron, Ontario, Michigan, Erie, Superior

5. <u>Ca</u>lcium, Calculator, Calico; <u>Gar</u>goyle, Garlic, Garnish; <u>Fan</u>cy, Fandango, Fantastic; <u>Com</u>edy, Common, Company; <u>Men</u>ace, Mendacious, Mental

6. Success, Argument, Pitcher, Absolute, Separate, Analyze, Graphic, Age Smart Age Happy

7. *Example:*

√ A <u>couple</u> traveling <u>abroad</u>, seated at an <u>outdoor</u> <u>café</u>, ordered a <u>roast</u> <u>duck</u>, listened to a strolling <u>musician</u> play a <u>violin</u> and watched the <u>birds</u> perched in the <u>trees.</u>

√√ A <u>couple</u> traveling <u>abroad</u>, seated at an <u>outdoor</u> <u>café</u>, drank <u>wine,</u> ordered a <u>roast duck</u>, listened to a strolling <u>musician</u> play a <u>violin</u> and watched the <u>birds</u> perched in the <u>trees</u> build their <u>nest</u>.

√√√ A <u>couple</u> traveling <u>abroad</u>, seated at an <u>outdoor</u> <u>café</u> in <u>France</u>, drank <u>wine</u> ordered a <u>roast</u> <u>duck</u> with <u>rice</u>, listened to a strolling <u>musician</u> play a <u>violin</u> and watched the <u>birds</u> perched in the <u>trees</u> near the <u>fountain</u> build their <u>nest</u>.

<u>CONSCIOUS RECALL</u>

2. *Dinner Table Items* Table cloth and napkins; Candles; Carving utensils; Serving utensils, Platters; Fish, salad, dinner, and desert forks; Fish, butter and service knifes; Soup and desert spoons; Bread and butter plates; Salad, service and cake plates; Soup bowls; Cups and saucers; Wine carafe; White and red wine glasses; Water glasses, Salt cellar, Pepper mill

3. *Desk Items* Blotter, Pens, Pencils, Holders, Clips, Stapler, Message Pad, Telephone, Calendar, Pads, Computer, Dictionary, Thesaurus, Message Machine, Glue, Paste, Tape, Rulers, Markers, Correction Fluid, Sharpener, Lamp, Folders

4. $1- George Washington; $5- Abraham Lincoln; $10- Alexander Hamilton; $20- Andrew Jackson; $50- Ulysses S. Grant; $100- Benjamin Franklin

5. *Capitals and Countries*

√

		√√	
London	England	Lisbon	Portugal
Madrid	Spain	Athens	Greece
Brussels	Belgium	Berlin	Germany
Rome	Italy	Cairo	Egypt
Washington	U.S.	Baghdad	Iraq
Ottawa	Canada	Ankara	Turkey
Copenhagen	Denmark	Moscow	Russia
		Cape Town	South Africa

√√√

Bern	Switzerland
Rabat	Morocco
Tehran	Iran
Brasilia	Brazil
Vienna	Austria
Prague	Czech Republic
Havana	Cuba
Jerusalem	Israel
Lima	Peru
Beijing	China

BIBLIOGRAPHY

Argyle, M. *The Psychology of Happiness.* UK: Routledge, 2001.

Benson, H. *The Relaxation Response.* NY: William Morrow, 1975.

Bragdon, A. & Gamon, D. *Use It or Lose It.* MA: Bragdon, 2000.

Butler, G. & Hope, T. *Managing Your Mind.* U.S.A.: Oxford U. Press, 1995.

Carlsen, M. *Creative Aging.* NY: Norton, 1991.

Carter, R. *Maximize Your Brain Power.* UK: John Wiley, 2002.

Chafetz, M. *Smart for Life.* NY: Penguin, 1992.

Chopra, Deepak. *Ageless Body, Timeless Mind.* NY: Crown, 1994.

Claflin, E., ed. *Age Protectors: Stop Aging Now.* PA: Rodale Press, 1998.

Csikszenthmihalyi, M. *Finding Flow.* NY: BasicBooks, 1997.

Cusack, D. & Thompson, W. *Mental Fitness for Life.* CO: Bull, 2005.

Damasio, A. *Descartes' Error.* NY: Putnam, 1994.

Evans, W. & Rosenberg, I. *Biomarkers.* NY: Simon & Schuster, 1991.

Goldman, B. *et al. Brain Fitness.* NY: Broadway, 1999.

Hayflick, L. *How and Why We Age.* NY: Ballentine Books, 1994.

Hodgson, H. *Smart Aging.* U.S.A.: John Wiley, 1999.

Hudson, F. *The Adult Years.* San Francisco: Jossey-Bass, 1999.

Katz, L & Rubin, M. *Keep Your Brain Alive.* NY:
    Workman, 1999.
Klein, S. *The Science of Happiness.* NY: Marlowe, 2002.
Layard, R. *Happiness: Lessons from a New Science.*
    NY: Penguin, 2005.
Lykken, D. *Happiness.* NY: St. Martin's, Griffin, 2000.
National Institute on Aging. (2001) *Exercise.*
    Washington, DC: U.S. Government Printing Office.
 Perlmutter, D. & Colman, C. *The Better Brain Book.*
    NY: Penguin, 2004.
Pinker, S. *How the Mind Works.* NY: Norton, 1997.
Restak, M.D., R.
    2001 Mozart's Brain and the Fighter Pilot. NY:
    Harmony.
    2006 *The Naked Brain.* NY: Harmony.
Rowe, J. & Kahn, R. *Successful Aging.* NY: Pantheon,
    1998.
Schmerl, E.& Tubach, S. *The Challenge of Age.* NY:
    Crossroad, 1991.
Seligman, M.
    2002 *Authentic Happiness.* NY: Free Press.
    2006 *Learned Optimism.* NY: Vintage.
Shankle, W. & Amen, D. *Preventing Alzheimer's.* NY:
    Penguin, 2004.
Snowdon, D. *Aging with Grace.* NY: Bantam, 2001.
Ullis, K. *Age Right.* NY: Fireside, 2000.
U.S. Dept. HHS. (2005). *Dietary Guidelines for
    Americans.* Washington, DC: U.S. Government
    Printing Office.
Vaillant, G. *Aging Well.* Boston: Little, Brown, 2002.
Weil, A. *Healthy Aging.* NY: Random House, 2005.
Whitbourne, S. *Adult Development and Aging.* U.S.:
    John Wiley, 2001.
Woodruff-Pak, D. *The Neuropsychology of Aging.* UK:
    Blackwell, 1997.

QUICK ORDER FORM

) Telephone Orders: 413.637.4036.

Fax Orders: 413.637.4036. Send this form.

Email Orders: agesmart@agesmart.us
Online Orders: www.agesmart.us Print and mail this form.

Postal Orders: Age Smart, Dr. Harriet Vines, PO Box 561, Lenox, MA 01240, USA

___Please send ____ copy/ies of *Age Smart* @ *$13.95* = $_____
___Please send FREE information about

      □ Speaking/Seminars
      □ Consulting

Name _____

Address _____

City_____State: _____ Zip: _____

Tele-
phone_____

Email _____

Sales tax: Please add 5.0% for products shipped to Massachusetts addresses.

Shipping by air
    U.S.: $4.00 for first item and $2.00 for each additional product.
    International: $9.00 for first item; $5.00 for each additional product (estimate).

Total Enclosed $_____ Payment by check or money order only.

QUICK ORDER FORM

) Telephone Orders: 413.637.4036.

📠 Fax Orders: 413.637.4036. Send this form.

💻 Email Orders: agesmart@agesmart.us
   Online Orders: www.agesmart.us Print and mail this form.

📠 Postal Orders: Age Smart, Dr. Harriet Vines, PO Box 561, Lenox, MA 01240, USA

___Please send ____ copy/ies of *Age Smart* @ *$13.95* = $_____
___Please send FREE information about

- □ Speaking/Seminars
- □ Consulting

Name _____

Address _____

City_____State: _____ Zip: _____

Tele-
phone_____

Email _____

Sales tax: Please add 5.0% for products shipped to Massachusetts addresses.

Shipping by air
   U.S.: $4.00 for first item and $2.00 for each additional product.
   International: $9.00 for first item; $5.00 for each additional product (estimate).

Total Enclosed $_____ Payment by check or money order only.

LaVergne, TN USA
04 November 2009

163024LV00003B/164/P